To Jack:

In celebration of your
birth!

Best wishes from The
Buchan family,

the Goodnight Book

for moms
AND
little ones

the Goodnight

Book

for moms AND little ones

Edited by *Alice Wong* and *Lena Tabori*

Designed by *Naomi Irie*

welcome
BOOKS

NEW YORK ★ SAN FRANCISCO

CONTENTS

CONTENTS

"*Sleep, sleep, my love, my only . . .* Be not afraid and be not lonely!" sings Charlotte the spider to Wilbur the pig, sending him gently and swiftly into dreamland. If only bedtime were always so easy! But it will come. My little ones are two, six, and eight. Now, the sweetest time I have with them is walking into their shared bedroom and seeing them asleep: Chi Chi with her soft snoring, Sylvia with her long limbs in every direction, and Phoebe with her little hands tucked under her cheek. Often I sneak into one of their beds for a snuggle. My second-favorite time is when they are all tucked in and awaiting their bedtime treat—a story, song, or poem. (Ah ... end of day, teeth brushed, children calm, mom's duties almost done ...) This is a quiet ritual we all look forward to—the girls have my attention, and I get to rest on the couch without them charging around, wrestling each other, or moving furniture.

A story is standard. Sylvia, my "girly girl," loves fairy tales. She thinks of herself as a princess, and tales like *The Princess and the Pea* are perfect for her. (We went through a "my bed isn't comfortable" stage.) Chi Chi is a reader now, and I am so excited to revisit the literary classics with her. In these pages, you and your little ones will discover mini-treasures—excerpts from well-loved books about sleep, dreams, and stars. There are also legends from various cultures about the origination of the moon, sky, stars, and dreams to satisfy curious young minds. Every once in a while, I like reading a poem to my kids ... the singsong verses soothe revved-up young minds. Poems by Eugene Field and Robert Louis Stevenson are old favorites, while Shel Silverstein's poetry, which I did not grow up with, is a new delight. Reading stories and poems does not always hold the attention of Phoebe because she is so young, but songs always capture her. And even though my voice hovers somewhere between passable and horrible, it is fun to try the hard notes on a somewhat forgiving, giggly audience.

I know a lot of moms are thinking that a happy, peaceful bedtime sounds too good to be true. I admit it is not always the case. Children go through many stages of resistance and fear of sleep. I've had and will continue to deal with my share of sobs, nightmares, and frequent visits into the children's bedroom. I find that consistency, boundaries, patience, and a no-nonsense attitude usually work. Try reading the Tips for Mom on page 67. It also helps to extend bedtime-related activities to include more than simply books and lullabies. Tucking your children in with a homemade glow-in-the-dark lamp shade by their side or a nighttime toy friend on their pillow can work wonders for a good night's rest. Teach your children to look forward to dreams with some of the dream activities. Perhaps some sleepy scents will do the trick. A gentle prayer also can help children feel safe and secure.

If your children still have difficulty falling asleep, take a look at their pre-bedtime diet. Read the information about foods on page 42 and try some of the sleep-encouraging recipes in this book. Or entice them with an occasional treat like Overnight Surprise Cookies on page 138—the cookies bake overnight in a cooling oven.

"And that's all there is..." as Miss Clavel says in *Madeleine* as she turns out the lights. And there is *plenty* here in this magical, wonderful book. I wish you and your children good night and sweet dreams.

—Alice Wong, Editor

The Land of Nod

From breakfast on all through the day
At home among my friends I stay;
But every night I go abroad
Afar into the land of Nod.

All by myself I have to go,
With none to tell me what to do—
All alone beside the streams
And up the mountainsides of dreams.

The strangest things are there for me,
Both things to eat and things to see,
And many frightening sights abroad
Till morning in the land of Nod.

Try as I like to find the way,
I never can get back by day,
Nor can remember plain and clear
The curious music that I hear.

—Robert Louis Stevenson

Charlotte's Web

Tired from his romp, Wilbur lay down in the clean straw. He closed his eyes. The straw seemed scratchy—not as comfortable as the cow manure, which was always delightfully soft to lie in. So he pushed the straw to one side and stretched out in the manure. Wilbur sighed. It had been a busy day—his first day of being terrific. Dozens of people had visited his yard during the afternoon, and he had had to stand and pose, looking as terrific as he could. Now he was tired. Fern had arrived and seated herself quietly on her stool in the corner.

"Tell me a story, Charlotte!" said Wilbur, as he lay waiting for sleep to come. "Tell me a story!"

So Charlotte, although she, too, was tired, did what Wilbur wanted…Charlotte told him about a cousin of hers who was an aeronaut.

"What is an aeronaut?" asked Wilbur.

"A balloonist," said Charlotte. "My cousin used to stand on her head and let out enough thread to form a balloon. Then she'd let go and be lifted into the air and carried upward on the warm wind."

"Is that true?" asked Wilbur. "Or are you just making it up?"

"It's true," replied Charlotte. "I have some very remarkable cousins. And now, Wilbur, it's time you went to sleep."

"Sing something!" begged Wilbur, closing his eyes.

So Charlotte sang a lullaby, while crickets chirped in the grass and the barn grew dark. This was the song she sang.

"Sleep, sleep, my love, my only,

Deep, deep, in the dung and the dark;

Be not afraid and be not lonely!

This is the hour when frogs and thrushes

Praise the world from the woods and the rushes.

Rest from care, my one and only,

Deep in the dung and the dark!"

But Wilbur was already asleep. When the song ended, Fern got up and went home.

HUSH LITTLE BABY

Hush little baby, don't say a word,
Papa's gonna buy you a mockingbird.

If that mockingbird won't sing,
Papa's gonna buy you a diamond ring.

If that diamond ring turns to brass,
Papa's gonna buy you a looking glass.

If that looking glass gets broke,
Papa's gonna buy you a billy goat.

If that billy goat don't pull,
Papa's gonna buy you a cart and bull.

If that cart and bull turn over,
Papa's gonna buy you a dog named Rover.

If that dog named Rover don't bark,
Papa's gonna buy you a horse and cart.

If that horse and cart fall down,
You'll still be the sweetest little baby in town.

Sleeping Beauty

O nce upon a time, there lived a wise King and kind Queen in a magic land. One day, the Queen gave birth to her first child, a daughter, and named her Bella, which means "beautiful." The King wished to have his baby daughter blessed by each of the ten fairies that lived in their land, and sent a messenger to invite them all to a celebration in honor of Bella's birth.

Though he searched beneath each rock and climbed up every tree, the messenger could find only nine of the fairies. The King did not want to leave any of the fairies out, but the tenth fairy was nowhere to be found.

On the day of the celebration, the entire kingdom was full of joy and happiness. Beaming with pride, the royal family presented their daughter, swathed in the finest silk and lace, to their guests. One by one, each fairy stepped forward and blessed Bella with a gift: not only would Bella have eternal beauty, she would also be intelligent, compassionate, and creative. The fairies blessed her with a wonderful sense of humor, perfect health, an adventurous spirit, and a kind heart.

Just as the ninth fairy stepped forward to bestow her blessing, a loud commotion was heard from the back of the hall. Suddenly, a very old fairy pushed her way through the crowd till she stood right in front of the King and Queen.

"How dare you not invite me to bless your firstborn child?! You disgust me!" she spat at the royal couple.

"But of course you were invited," said the shocked King, "we searched high and low, but couldn't find you anywhere!"

"Lies!" accused the fairy, "you're full of lies! Well, I shall make you pay for your insult by giving your daughter a very special blessing." With that, the old fairy placed her hand on the Princess's forehead and uttered, "I, the fairy of mortality, decree that this child will prick her finger on a spindle in her sixteenth year and fall dead in an instant, along with any living thing inside these castle walls." The Queen let out an anguished sob.

"Maybe," snapped the old fairy as she left the room, "you'll think better next time before you show me such discourtesy!"

Just then, the ninth fairy stepped forward and offered sympathetically, "My dear King and Queen, I cannot undue this terrible curse, but I can temper it." The fairy placed a hand on baby Bella's head and continued, "Do not let this child, nor any other living soul, die by the prick of a spindle, but fall fast asleep for a hundred years, instead."

The King thanked the fairy for her kindness, and further decreed that all the sewing spindles in his kingdom be taken away and burned to ashes.

Years passed, and Princess Bella grew to be a gentle, kind, intelligent, and beautiful young woman. On her sixteenth birthday, her parents threw her an extravagant party and invited all the people in the land to join them in their celebration. That night, the princess danced her heart out with almost every young man in the kingdom. As the last song of the night was announced, a dashing prince tapped Bella lightly on the shoulder. "Your Highness," he asked politely, "may I have this dance?"

As Bella whirled around to answer, she was stunned by the sight of the young prince standing before her.

"Why, I would be honored," she replied with a curtsy.

As the couple waltzed, the dance floor slowly cleared, the other guests unable to do any—

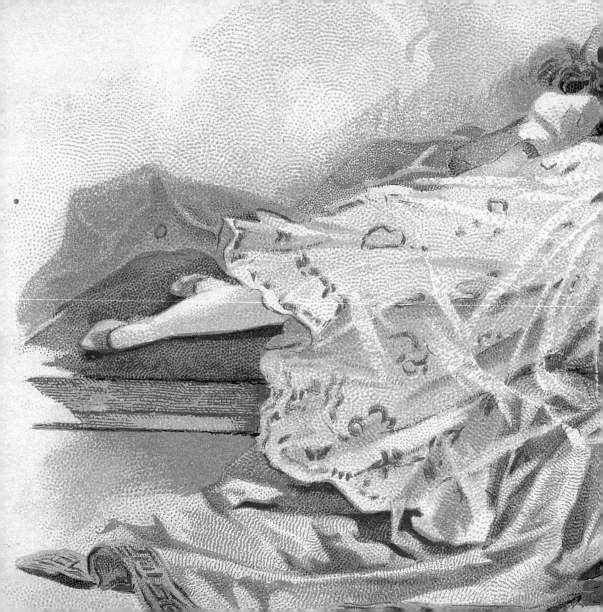

thing but stop and stare at the graceful pair. The dance seemed to end too soon, and the Prince asked Bella if he could call on her again. She readily agreed, and watched as he rode off into the night.

Her parents had seen how joyful the Princess and Prince looked together, and decided to visit the Prince's kingdom and talk with his parents about a possible marriage. While they were gone, Bella could hardly sit still—she was so nervous and excited! She decided to explore a tower in the castle that had always been declared "off limits" to her. As she climbed the narrow staircase leading to the tower's uppermost room, the Princess heard a soft clicking that grew louder as she approached the top step. Cautiously, she opened a heavy wooden door and discovered an old woman sitting at a spindle, quietly sewing some linens. As Bella approached her, the old lady looked up and smiled. "Would you like to try my spindle?" she asked kindly.

Bella quickly agreed and walked toward the spindle. But as she sat down, her pinkie finger grazed the spindle's needle and she felt a tiny prick. Immediately, the Princess's eyelids drooped and she fell slowly off the stool, landing softly on the floor. The sleeping spell spread quickly throughout the castle, and every scullery maid, cook, courtier, knight, dog, cat, and goldfish fell fast asleep where they stood (or swam!). The old fairy's curse had finally come true, and the beautiful Princess, along with her royal staff, were to lay sleeping for a hundred years.

The King and Queen wept bitterly when they learned of their daughter's fate. They decided to leave the castle just as it was, frozen in time, so that when the Princess awoke she would feel at home.

The years passed and time went forward, except in Bella's castle. A legend was born that the most beautiful princess in the world lay fast asleep in one of the stone towers, and that the fairies looked in on her every evening. But no one ever dared enter it, fearing they too would fall under the fairy's spell.

One day, a handsome young Prince arrived at the castle. Although he had been warned about the mysterious curse, the Prince had heard the tale of the sleeping Princess and had come to see her with his own eyes. He gathered his courage and strode boldly across the drawbridge. At that moment the curse was lifted, for exactly one century had gone by since the Princess pricked her finger on the spindle. The Prince climbed the staircase to the tower and found Princess Bella still asleep. He knelt over her, gently lifted her head, and kissed her tenderly on the lips. "Wake up my sleeping beauty, wake up," he whispered.

The Princess's eyes fluttered open and she saw above her a man who looked just like the Prince she had fallen in love with a hundred years before. You see, this was the great great great grandson of the Prince who had stolen Bella's heart on her sixteenth birthday.

Bella yawned and smiled at the young Prince. "I must have fallen asleep while I was sewing. Am I to be your bride?"

"Oh I hope so," replied the love-struck Prince. "But I am not the man you think I am." And he told the Princess of how long she had slept and how the world had both changed and stayed the same while she'd been slumbering.

The Princess was confused at first, and quite heartbroken to hear of her parents' deaths. But in time, she became happy again, as she once had been. She fell deeply in love with the Prince who had woken her, just as she had with his great great great grandfather. Before long, the Prince and Princess married and lived happily ever after in their castle. ✳

DREAMY

Cosmic nightshirts are comfortable, fun, and they glow in the dark! They're a great project to try out at sleepovers or anytime. Slipper socks are a snap to make and will send your toes straight to dreamland as soon as you slip them on. And if you want to make sure you really get a good night's rest, a sleep mask will keep it dark enough for you to snooze all night long.

Cosmic Nightshirt

Newspaper, large white cotton T-shirt (clean and unwrinkled), cardboard sheet, sponges cut into different astral shapes (like moons and stars), fluorescent washable fabric paint, paper plate, paintbrush

1. Lay down newspaper to catch any drips.
2. Slip a sheet of cardboard into the T-shirt. This will make sure no paint bleeds to the back.
3. Pour some paint on a paper plate. Firmly press a sponge shape into the paint, making sure all areas on one side are covered.
4. Decorate your nightshirt by pressing the sponge slowly and carefully against the fabric. Use different colors and different-size sponges.
5. Add words or more shapes with the paintbrush. Let dry overnight before wearing.
6. To make sure your design doesn't fade after washing, wait 24 hours, then turn the shirt inside out and go over the design with an iron on medium heat. Or you could tumble dry your shirt for about 30 minutes in your clothes dryer.

SLEEPWEAR

Slipper Socks

1 pair thick cotton socks, puffy fabric paint, felt, needle, thread, scissors (optional)

1. Lay the socks with the bottom sides up. Use puffy paint to draw dots, lines, zigzags or any design on the sole. These will make the socks nonskid.
2. Let socks dry for at least a day before wearing.
3. For cool glowing footwear, use black or dark socks and decorate with fluorescent puffy paint.
4. For a cute and cuddly pair of pals gazing up at you, cut out 4 felt ears and sew on each side of the sock cuffs. Use paint to add eyes and noses for snuggly bunnies, puppies, or kittens!

Sleep Mask

Blue felt, marker, scissors, yellow felt, fabric glue, 1/8- to 1/4- inch-wide elastic in a length that will comfortably fit around your head, needle, thread

1. Place two pieces of blue felt together. The felt should be wide enough to fit face. Draw the shape shown in *figure a* with a marker. Carefully cut the outline on the felt.
2. On one blue felt, draw moons, stars, and comets. Cut out the shapes. Set aside.
3. Draw and cut out the same *figure a* shape on yellow felt, making it slightly smaller than the blue felt shapes.

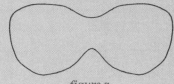

figure a

4. Sandwich the yellow piece of felt between the two blue pieces.
5. Carefully squeeze fabric glue around the edge of one blue piece and press it firmly to the other blue piece, keeping the yellow felt in the middle.
6. Ask an adult to sew the elastic to the mask about one inch from each side.

The Seven Star Brothers

*Sometimes, on a clear night, you can see seven little stars all clustered together.
This is the constellation called the Pleiades, and here is an interesting story of how they came to be.*

Once, a long time ago, seven brothers were wandering through the world on their own. They didn't know where their parents were, and they had only one another. Every day they had to hunt for food, and each night they had to shelter themselves against the wind, rain, and wild animals. It was a hard life.

One fall day, the littlest brother stopped by a pond to play with some drifting leaves. He told his brothers, "I am very tired of moving around so much. Why can't we just stay in one place?"

The middle brother told him, "Because the wild animals might find us. Winter is coming soon, and we don't want to get caught in the snow, do we? We have to keep moving."

The little brother thought about this and then said, "What if we all make a wish to be something else? If we wish hard enough, maybe we will change. That way we won't have to worry about animals finding us, or the weather giving us colds, or always being so hungry."

All the brothers agreed this was a good idea. They began to think about the best thing to become. As they thought, they walked on until they came to a rushing, roaring river. Although it was not deep, the water was cold and ran very swiftly. They managed to swim across, but they were all exhausted and freezing when they flopped down on the other side.

"I know!" exclaimed one brother, "Why don't we wish to be water? Water is powerful

and swift! No enemy could catch us!"

The wisest brother shook his head. "Water dries up in the summer. Do you want to dry up?"

Nobody wanted that, so the brothers continued to think of what to become.

The next day as they made their way through a forest, a huge bear suddenly lumbered from behind a tree. He chased the brothers for a long time before they managed to escape him.

"That was close!" One brother said. "Hey, why don't we become bears? We'd be so big and strong, no one would mess with us then!"

The wisest brother answered, "But men would hunt us. We would still feel the cold of winter."

The brothers traveled on, and soon they came to a rocky mountain. It was difficult making their way over the boulders strewn in their path, and they were soon tired from climbing up the steep slope.

When they stopped to rest, one brother suggested, "Why don't we become the land? No one hunts the land. We would be safe in the ground."

But the wise brother replied, "The rain soaks into the ground and changes it. Earthquakes move the rocks around. Plants push their way through it. The earth does not stay the same."

They all thought about the changes the earth underwent, and realized the wise brother was again correct.

"Well, if we can't be the land, maybe we can be something that grows from the land," said one optimistic brother as he climbed a nearby tree. "What about a tall tree? They stay the same for ages and ages!"

This time, the wisest one didn't even need to speak. The middle brother piped up, "What happens to trees every season? Their leaves change color, then fall. Their trunks grow gnarled. Big storms can knock them down." All the brothers thought about how the seasons changed the trees, and knew this was true.

The seven brothers came up with many other suggestions, but none of them seemed right. Night seemed like a good choice at first, but then someone brought up the fact that day is always chasing it, never letting it rest.

All at once, the littlest brother leapt up and danced with excitement. "But nothing ever changes for the stars!" he told his brothers. "They are there forever and ever. Sometimes you can even see them very faintly during the day. Let us all wish really hard to change into stars, and then we will be together and safe forever and ever."

Everyone agreed this was a wonderful plan. They carefully climbed to the top of the highest mountain and wished with all of their might to turn into stars. Suddenly, a silvery ladder appeared in the sky. They looked at each other and noticed they had all begun to glow. The seven brothers knew they had gotten their wish, so they laughed and climbed the ladder up to the sky. And there they sit to this day, seven brothers all happy and safe, looking down and smiling at the world below.

Star Light

Did you know that there are about eight thousand stars you can see from Earth without a telescope? Many of these stars make up constellations, like the Great Bear or Orion, and your very own star gazer can help you recognize some of these starry pictures. Glimpse a group of these twinkling lights in the middle of the day by making a constellation chart. And you can even watch falling stars any time you like with a beautiful starry-night snow globe.

Star Gazer

Star chart, aluminum foil, straight pins, 2-liter plastic soda bottle, scissors, black construction paper, tape, penlight

1. Place the star chart over the shiny side of a piece of aluminum foil. With a straight pin, poke a tiny hole through each major star so that the pin goes through the foil. When you're done, the foil should be a replica of the major stars in your star chart.
2. Ask an adult to help you cut the bottom off the soda bottle. Wrap the bottle in construction paper and tape it in place.
3. Cover the bottom of the soda bottle with the aluminum foil. Make sure that the shiny side of the foil faces the inside of the bottle. Tape the foil in place.
4. Look through the mouth of the bottle. The pinpricks of light should be a good representation of the night sky. Try shining a penlight through the mouth of the bottle in a dark room and casting your stars against the wall. Not only will your star gazer bring the glowing cosmos into your house, but it will also help you recognize the constellation in the real night sky.

STAR BRIGHT

Constellation Chart

Black construction paper, colored chalk, safety pin, glue stick, glitter, tape

1. Choose a constellation that you like. See pages 214—221 to learn about some good ones.
2. On the black construction paper, use chalk to draw the constellation. Use dashed lines to make the outline of the starry figure.
3. Make dots where large stars or planets appear in your constellation.
4. Carefully use a safety pin to punch through the dots. Wiggle it a little bit to make the holes a little bigger.
5. Use the glue stick to spread a thin layer of glue over the dashed line outline. Then sprinkle with glitter. Wait for it to dry and then shake off excess glitter.
6. Label your constellation using chalk.
7. Tape your picture to a window. When light shines through your picture, the pinpricks will light up and you'll be able to see a starry outline of your constellation!

Starry-Night Snow Globe

Glass or plastic jar with a wide mouth and tightly fitting lid, aluminum foil, glow-in-the-dark tape (optional), glitter, distilled water, dishwashing liquid, black electrical tape

1. Wash the jar and remove any labels.
2. Mold a crescent-moon shape out of the aluminum foil. If you wish, cover it in glow-in-the-dark tape. Put the moon in the jar.
3. Sprinkle glitter into the jar until the bottom is covered.
4. Fill the jar with distilled water all the way to the top. Add a drop of dishwashing liquid to the water to make sure it doesn't get cloudy or moldy.
5. Screw the lid on tightly and wrap a piece of black electrical tape around the bottom to make sure the lid doesn't come off.
6. To have a starry night any time, turn the jar over and gently shake.

When You Wish Upon a Star

By Leigh Harline and Ned Washington

When a star is born,
They possess a gift or two,
One of them is this
They have the power
To make a wish come true.

When you wish upon a star,
Makes no diff'rence who you are,
Anything your heart desires
will come to you.

If your heart is in your dream,
No request is too extreme,
When you wish upon a star
as dreamers do.

Fate is kind,
She brings to those who love,
The sweet fulfillment of their
secret longing.

Like a bolt out of the blue,
Fate steps in and sees you thru,
When you wish upon a star
Your dream comes true.

Mary Poppins
P. L. Travers

There was the sound of a front door being quietly opened and shut again, and the creak of footsteps on the path. Mrs. Corry smiled and waved her hand as Mary Poppins came to meet them, carrying a market basket on her arm, and in the basket was something that seemed to give out a faint, mysterious light.

"Come along, come along, we must hurry! We haven't much time," said Mrs. Corry, taking Mary Poppins by the arm. "Look lively, you two!" And she moved off, followed by Miss Fannie and Miss Annie, who were obviously trying to look as lively as possible but not succeeding very well. They tramped heavily after their Mother and Mary Poppins, bending under their loads.

Jane and Michael saw all four of them go down Cherry-Tree Lane, and then they turned a little to the left and went up the hill. When they got to the top of the hill, where there were no houses but only grass and clover, they stopped.

Miss Annie put down her pail of glue, and Miss Fannie swung the ladders from her shoulder and steadied them until both stood in an upright position. Then she held one and Miss Annie the other.

"What on earth are they going to do?" said Michael, gaping.

But there was no need for Jane to reply, for he could see for himself what was happening.

As soon as Miss Fannie and Miss Annie had so fixed the ladders that they seemed to be standing with one end on the earth and the other leaning on the sky, Mrs. Corry picked up her skirts and the paint-brush in one hand and the pail of glue in the other. Then she set her foot on the lowest rung of one of the ladders and began to climb it. Mary Poppins, carrying her basket, climbed the other.

Then Jane and Michael saw a most amazing sight. As soon as she arrived at the top of her ladder, Mrs. Corry dipped her brush into the glue and began slapping the sticky substance against the sky. And Mary Poppins, when this had been done, took something shiny from her basket and fixed it to the glue. When she took her hands away they saw that she was sticking the Gingerbread Stars to the sky. As each one was placed in position it began to twinkle furiously, sending out rays of sparkling golden light.

"They're ours!" said Michael breathlessly. "They're our stars. She thought we were asleep and came in and took them!"

But Jane was silent. She was watching Mrs. Corry splashing the glue on the sky and Mary Poppins sticking on the stars and Miss Fannie and Miss Annie moving the ladders to a new position as the spaces in the sky became filled up.

At last it was over. Mary Poppins shook out her basket and showed Mrs. Corry that there was nothing left in it. Then they came down from the ladders and the procession started down the hill again, Miss Fannie shouldering the ladders, Miss Annie jangling her empty pail of glue. At the corner they stood talking for a moment; then Mary Poppins shook hands with them all and hurried up the Lane again. Mrs. Corry, dancing lightly in her elastic-sided boots and holding her skirts daintily with her hands, disappeared in the other direction with her huge daughters stumping noisily behind her.

The garden-gate clicked. Footsteps creaked on the path. The front door opened and shut with a soft clanging sound. Presently they heard Mary Poppins come quietly up the stairs, tip-toe past the nursery and go on into the room where she slept with John and Barbara.

As the sound of her footsteps died away, Jane and Michael looked at each other. Then without a word they went together to the top left-hand drawer and looked.
There was nothing there but a pile of Jane's handkerchiefs.

"I told you so," said Michael.

Next they went to the wardrobe and looked into the shoe-box. It was empty.

"But how? But why?" said Michael, sitting down on the edge of his bed and staring at Jane.

Jane said nothing. She just sat beside him with her arms round her knees and thought and thought and thought. At last she shook back her hair and stretched herself and stood up.

"What I want to know," she said, "is this: Are the stars gold paper or is the gold paper stars?"

There was no reply to her question and she did not expect one. She knew that only somebody very much wiser than Michael could give her the right answer... ☾

*N*ow I lay me down to sleep,
I pray Thee, Lord, thy child to keep:
Thy love guard me through the night
And wake me with the morning light.

—*Traditional*

*N*ow that the sun has set,
I sit and rest, and think of you.
Give my weary body peace.
Let my legs and arms stop aching,
Let my nose stop sneezing,
Let my head stop thinking.
Let me sleep in your arms.

—*Dinka*

The Pied Piper of Hamelin

Once upon a time the village of Hamelin sat upon the banks of a great river. The people who lived there considered themselves lucky, for they were all rich, ate the finest foods, wore the most stylish clothes, and lived in the most elegant houses. But even so, Hamelin had a big problem: rats—mean, gray rats with sharp, gray teeth everywhere you looked. These rats were very smart, and they never walked into the traps or ate the poison the villagers set out for them. Instead, they nibbled on food, clothing, and even toes! Determined to find a solution, the people of Hamelin went straight to the mayor.

"LET'S GET CATS TO KILL THE RATS!" the mayor proposed.

Everyone cheered, proud that they had elected such a firm and smart man.

Within a week, everyone in town had at least three cats. (They never bought just one of anything.)

For two weeks, the mayor's plan worked splendidly. The cats ate the rats, and the people of Hamelin forgot their worries. But then something strange happened. The cats started dying and the rats started multiplying. Soon, there were more rats than ever—everywhere you looked! A meeting was called in the Town Hall.

"We've tried poison and traps," said a woman.

"And thousands of cats," said a man.

"How can we get rid of the rats?" the people cried out.

The mayor shrugged helplessly.

Suddenly, there was a knock at the door.

When the mayor's assistant opened it, a tall, thin stranger dressed in brightly colored silks entered the room. A long feather stuck out of his purple hat, and he carried a beautiful, golden pipe.

"I am the Pied Piper," the stranger said, "and I've freed other villages of beetles and bats. Pay me a thousand gold coins, and I'll get rid of all your rats!"

"We'll give you fifty thousand gold coins if you succeed!" said the mayor.

"Very well," said the Pied Piper. "By daybreak tomorrow, there won't be a rat left in Hamelin!" Then he was gone.

That evening at sunset, the magical tones of a pipe wafted through the village of Hamelin. Rats scampered out of every nook and cranny in every house, shop, and office, to flock at the heels of the Pied Piper. When he reached the river, the Pied Piper continued to play as he waded straight in. By the time the water reached his chest, all the rats had drowned and every last one of them was swept away by the current.

"I'd like my fifty thousand gold coins," the Pied Piper told the mayor the next morning.

"Fifty thousand!" exclaimed the greedy mayor, for, though the village had money, it was needed to maintain the fancy gardens, parks, and museums. Now that the rats were gone, why pay the piper what he had promised, he reasoned; the town's problem had already been solved.

"Then give me a thousand gold coins, as I originally requested!" said the Piper, annoyed.

"I'll give you fifty," said the mayor, "which I think is very generous indeed."

The townspeople agreed, for they loved their gardens, parks, and museums. "You should simply be grateful for what you get," they said.

"You can keep your fifty measly gold coins!" cried the Piper. "You broke your promise, and you'll soon regret it." Then he disappeared.

That night, the people of Hamelin slept soundly, for they no longer worried about rats crawling into bed with them. When the sound of the Pied Piper's pipe wafted through the streets, only the children heard it. In their pajamas, the children of Hamelin—from toddlers to teenagers—left their houses and followed the Pied Piper to a dark forest at the edge of town, mesmerized by the magical tones of his pipe.

The Pied Piper led the procession through the forest to the foot of a majestic mountain. He played three mysterious notes, and a giant piece of the mountain creaked open like a door. In he marched, playing his golden pipe, with the children at his heels. When they were all inside, the mountain closed up behind them.

"Wait for me!" cried a boy with a twisted ankle, who hadn't been quick enough. But the door was nowhere to be found.

When the sun came up, the boy returned to the village of Hamelin, where everyone was looking for their children—including the mayor, whose eight sons and eight daughters had all disappeared during the night.

The boy with the twisted ankle told everyone what had happened. The mayor and the townspeople wailed and cried for their children, but it was no use.

The Pied Piper and the children of Hamelin were never seen again, and, to this day, no one has ever found an entrance to the mountain.

IF YOU ARE GETTING ENOUGH SLEEP AT NIGHT, you should feel tired only when you have had a long day of activity or your bedtime is rolling around. But sometimes you might find yourself yawning after you eat a certain meal. So what's the story? It might surprise you to know that sometimes it's the foods you eat that make you feel tired and sleepy. You can use these foods to help you relax at night and get your mind and body ready for an easy bedtime. Although that leftover piece of chocolate cake may seem tempting, the best bedtime snacks are ones that are low in sugar and contain sleep-inducing ingredients.

Why Some Foods Make You Sleepy

Your brain uses something called tryptophan, found in the foods you eat, to make chemicals in your body that cause you to go to sleep. Tryptophan is an amino acid found in foods that have a lot of protein, like turkey, eggs, nuts, and milk. However, protein also contains a lot of other amino acids, some of which can actually make you stay awake. When you eat a snack high only in protein, you might not get tired because the other amino acids are blocking the tryptophan and not allowing the sleepy effects to take hold. That is why it is necessary to eat complex carbohydrates along with your protein. Your body secretes the hormone insulin in response to eating complex carbohydrates, which raise blood sugar levels. Insulin holds back the amino acids that keep you awake and lets the sleep-inducing tryptophan enter the brain. It is important to eat a snack that is high in complex carbohydrates, but that also contains protein and even some calcium.

Snacks to Help You Snooze

Try one of these simple and soothing treats as a light snack to help you get to sleep. Some of the snacks work as part of a protein-high carbohydrate combination, and some are just naturally high in tryptophan.
★ Apple pie and milk ★ Cheese and crackers ★ Cottage cheese ★ English muffin with low-sugar jelly or jam ★ Fresh bananas ★ Glass of warm milk with a sprinkle of nutmeg and graham or animal crackers ★ Ice cream or sorbet ★ Soy milk or tofu ★ Whole-grain cereal with milk and

banana slices ★ Yogurt topped with granola or fresh fruit ★ Rice cakes with a smear of peanut butter ★ Apple sauce or apple slices

General Guidelines

The above foods work best if you eat them about an hour or two before you go to sleep, not right before. Your body needs time to digest and absorb the food into your system.

Big meals that are heavy and greasy may make you feel drowsy, but you shouldn't eat them right before going to sleep. Heavy meals can lead to an upset stomach or indigestion if you don't give yourself a chance to digest first. Keep the portions small and light.

Some people prefer eating bigger breakfasts and lunches, and then something light for dinner. That way they have plenty of time to digest before they go to sleep. Be careful though; an empty stomach can keep you awake just as much as a full one can.

If you cannot pair a protein-rich food, like turkey, with a complex carbohydrate, like whole-grain bread, it's better to eat the protein-rich food on an empty stomach.

Foods to Avoid

Just like foods that relax and calm you, there are also foods high in chemicals that make you feel energized and keep you awake. Although they might be a great boost for you first thing in the morning, stay away from them when you are trying to relax:

★ Bacon, ham, and sausage ★ Tomatoes ★ Peppers ★ Sugar and chocolate ★ Spicy treats

Of course, the biggest snooze-thief is caffeine. Caffeine causes your body system to speed up. Many doctors say you shouldn't eat or drink anything with caffeine in it after 5 P.M. to make sure you get a good night's rest. Easy places to find caffeine are in soft drinks, teas, coffee, and chocolate. If you drink or eat things that contain caffeine during the afternoon, make sure to drink lots of water in the evening to flush it out of your system. Substitute natural fruit juices, milk, or unsweetened, herbal iced tea for soft drinks. Not only will you sleep better, but they're healthier for your body, too!

Wynken,
Blynken, and Nod

Wynken, Blynken, and Nod one night
Sailed off in a wooden shoe—
Sailed on a river of crystal light,
Into a sea of dew.
"Where are you going, and what do you wish?"
The old moon asked the three.
"We have come to fish for the herring fish
That live in this beautiful sea;
Nets of silver and gold have we,"
Said Wynken,
Blynken,
And Nod.

The old moon laughed and sang a song,
As they rocked in the wooden shoe,
And the wind that sped them all night long
Ruffled the waves of dew.
The little stars were the herring fish
That lived in that beautiful sea;
"Now cast your nets wherever you wish,
Never afeared are we!"

So cried the stars to the fishermen three,
Wynken,
Blynken,
And Nod.

All night long their nets they threw
To the stars in the twinkling foam,
Then down from the sky came the wooden shoe,
Bringing the fishermen home.
'Twas all so pretty a sail, it seemed
As if it could not be;
And some folk thought 'twas a dream they'd dreamed
Of sailing that beautiful sea;
But I shall name you the fishermen three,
Wynken,
Blynken,
And Nod.

Wynken and Blynken are two little eyes,
And Nod is a little head,
And the wooden shoe that sailed the skies
Is a wee one's trundle bed.
So shut your eyes while Mother sings
Of wonderful sights that be,
And you shall see the beautiful things
As you rock in the misty sea
Where the old shoe rocked the fishermen three,
Wynken,
Blynken,
And Nod.

—*Eugene Field*

The

Little Prince

Antoine de Saint-Exupéry

People have stars, but they aren't the same. For travelers, the stars are guides. For other people, they're nothing but tiny lights. And for still others, for scholars, they're problems. For my businessman, they were gold. But all those stars are silent stars. You, though, you'll have stars like nobody else."

"What do you mean?"

"When you look up at the stars at night, since I'll be living on one of them, since I'll be laughing on one of them, for you it'll be as if all the stars are laughing. You'll have stars that can laugh!"

And he laughed again.

"And when you're consoled (everyone eventually is consoled), you'll be glad you've known me. You'll always be my friend. You'll feel like laughing with me. And you'll open your window sometimes just for the fun of it . . . And your friends will be amazed to see you laughing while you're looking up at the sky. Then you'll tell them, 'Yes, it's the stars; they always make me laugh!' And they'll think you're crazy. It'll be a nasty trick I played on you . . ."

And he laughed again.

"And it'll be as if I had given you, instead of stars, a lot of tiny bells that know how to laugh . . ." ☾

TWINKLE, TWINKLE, LITTLE STAR

By Jane Taylor

Twinkle, twinkle,
little star,
How I wonder
what you are!
Up above the world
so high,
Like a diamond
in the sky.

When the blazing
sun is gone,
When he nothing
shines upon,
Then you show
your little light,
Twinkle, twinkle
all the night.

Then the traveller
in the dark
Thanks you for
your tiny spark;
He could not see
which way to go,
If you did not twinkle so.

In the dark blue
sky you keep,
And often through
my curtains peep,
For you never
shut your eye,
'Til the sun is in the sky.

As your bright
and tiny spark
Lights the traveller
in the dark—
Though I know not
what you are,
Twinkle, twinkle,
little star.

Coyote and his star

Coyote always enjoyed watching the night sky. It was his favorite thing to do, besides playing tricks on people. He loved seeing the little stars flicker and sparkle as if they were dancing in the velvety black sky. Every night he would look at them. Sometimes he would even have conversations with them, but they didn't answer him back.

One night, Coyote noticed a certain star that was particularly beautiful. This star shone brighter and clearer then any other star in the sky. In fact, Coyote thought the star was so lovely that he fell in love with her! Instead of looking at all the stars, he looked only at the one. And instead of talking to all the stars, he spoke only to her. He asked her to come to earth to visit him. He begged her to say a kind word to him. But the beautiful star only danced in the sky, lovely and silent the entire time.

Coyote felt as if he would go crazy if he did not talk to the star. Looking off in the distance, he saw a very tall mountain that the star would almost touch each night. Immediately he set off for the mountain. It took many days, but when he arrived, he was very pleased. The top of the mountain was close to the stars.

That evening, when the stars appeared, Coyote waited for his star to glide by the mountain. He waved his arms and shouted up, "Dear Star, why won't you speak to me?"

The star looked confused. "Who said that?" she said. Then she looked at the mountain and saw a small, brown speck waving at her. "Oh, I didn't even see you down there. I'm sorry,

what did you say?"

Coyote shouted up, "I said, why won't you speak to me?"

"I'm a star. Sometimes I'm too far up to hear anything but the wind whistling through the night air." She started to move a little closer.

Coyote understood now. "Star, I think you are the most beautiful thing in the whole world. You are the most graceful dancer. Will you carry me up to the sky so that I can dance with you? Just once?" The star reached down one of her points, and Coyote grabbed on. Then he soared up and up and up into the night sky! He twirled and danced with the star all night. They dipped and whirled and swooped all over the sky. It was the most fun Coyote had ever had.

After they had been dancing for quite a while, Coyote began to feel tired. "Couldn't we take a rest?"

The star looked surprised. "What do you mean? I'm a star. I never need a rest."

Coyote looked down nervously. "Boy, it sure is a long way to the ground."

"I never notice," the star replied, "To me, the earth is always that far away."

Coyote's arms were starting to hurt from holding on to the star. "I think I'd better let go now. I've had enough dancing for one night."

The star shook her head. "But you can't let go. You'll fall for a week and a day before you touch the land. I love you and want to stay with you always."

Although Coyote was very glad to hear these words from such a beautiful star, his arms were getting extremely tired. Before he could even say good-bye, he slipped off and fell down, down, down, for a whole week and a day. When he hit the land, he made a big hole in the ground. Luckily, Coyote had a little bit of magic in him or he could have been badly hurt. He shook himself off and walked home. Coyote never again went up into the night sky to dance. But sometimes, on very clear nights, he would climb to the top of the big mountain, just so he could talk to his favorite star. ❁

NIGHTTIME

It's easier to go to sleep if you know someone's watching over you, or if you have a cuddly friend to snuggle with. Make a sweet little angel that you can clip above your pillow. Many animals hibernate during the winter to store up energy for the springtime, and if you're lucky, a beanbag bear might choose your bed to sleep the winter through.

Clothespin Guardian Angel

Colored tissue paper, glue, wooden clothespin, pipe cleaner, marker

1. Cut the tissue paper into a 5½-inch square. Fold back and forth in ½-inch segments so it looks like a fan. This will be the wings.
2. Pinch the center of the folded wings. Clamp the wings at the center with the clothespin. The clothespin forms the angel's body. You might want to add a drop of glue so the tissue paper stays put.

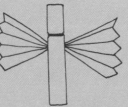

3. Gently unfold and fan out the outer edges of the wings to expand them.

4. Fold the pipe cleaner in half. Make a loop by twisting the pipe cleaner about ¼ inch from the bend. Bend the loop forward so it makes a right angle from the rest of the pipe cleaner. This will be the halo.

5. Wrap the pipe cleaner ends around the angel's waist. Twist the ends together around the front to make praying hands. Draw a face with marker.

Hibernating Beanbag Bear

16-inch square of brown felt or other soft fabric, straight pins, black marker, scissors, light brown or yellow felt, needle, thread to match fabric, dried beans

1. Fold the fabric in half and pin at the edges to hold.
2. Draw a bear shape on the fabric and carefully cut it out.

FRIENDS

3. Draw a nose, mouth, and a pair of sleepy eyes on the bear's head.

4. Cut out two small half circles for the bear's ears and a circle for the bear's tummy from the light brown or yellow felt.

5. Sew the ear and tummy pieces onto one of the two bear pieces.

6. Place the two pieces of fabric together with the bear's front facing down. Sew the edges together, leaving a large opening (at least 1½ inches) under the bear's arm for the beans. Keep the stitches close together to make sure no beans slip out.

7. Carefully turn the bear right side out, pulling it through the opening you left for the beans. Stuff a good amount of beans in the bear, but be careful not to overfill it. Sew the opening closed.

I'm Only Sleeping

By John Lennon and Paul McCartney

When I wake up early in the morning,
Lift my head, I'm still yawning,
When I'm in the middle of a dream,
Stay in bed, float upstream.

Please don't wake me, No, don't shake me,
Leave me where I am; I'm only sleeping.

Ev'rybody seems to think I'm lazy,
I don't mind, I think they're crazy,
Runnin' ev'rywhere at such a speed,
'Till they find there's no need.

Please don't spoil my day, I'm miles away,
And after all, I'm only sleeping.

Keeping an eye on the world going by my window,
Taking my time.
Lying there and staring at the ceiling,

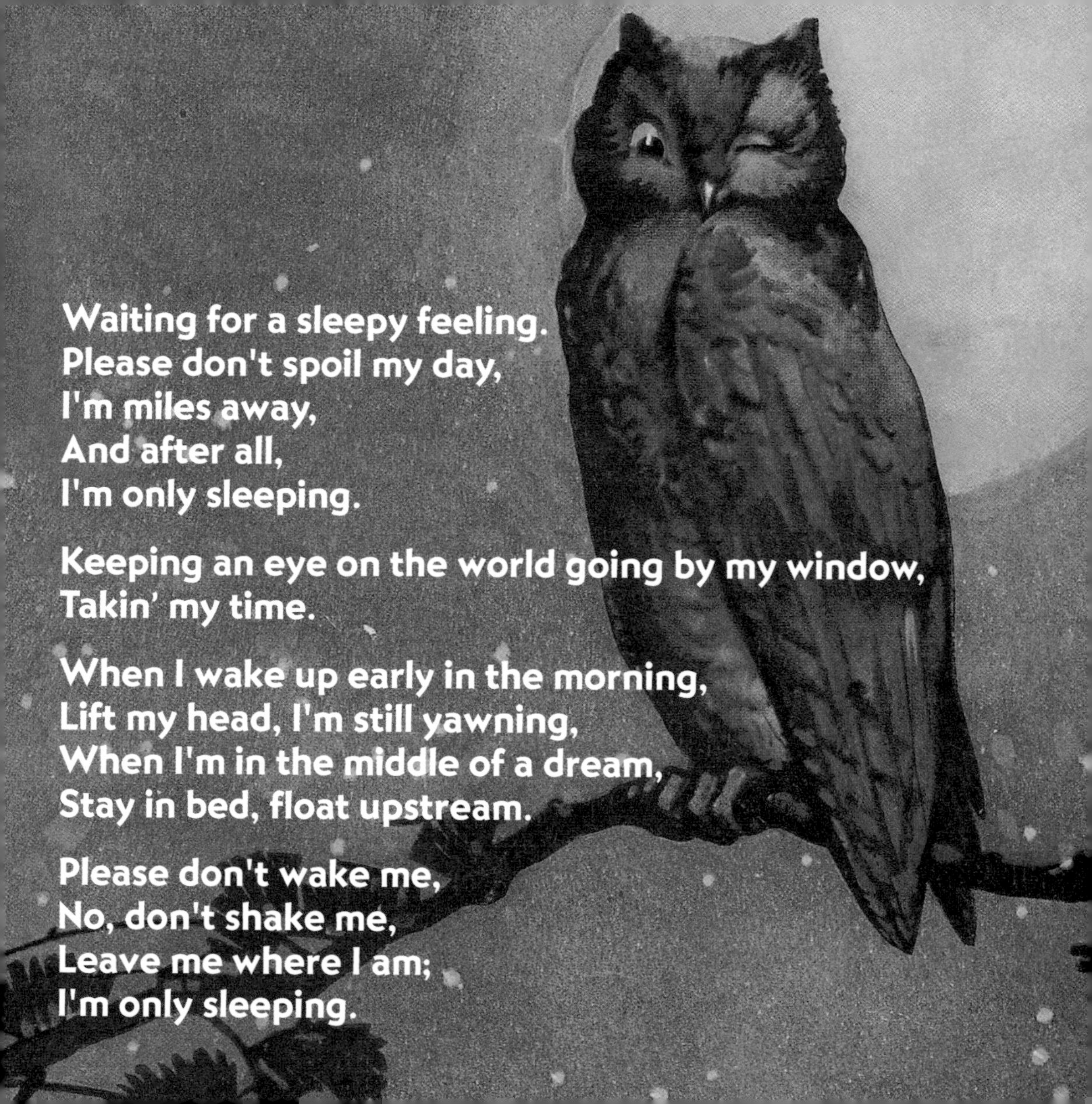

Waiting for a sleepy feeling.
Please don't spoil my day,
I'm miles away,
And after all,
I'm only sleeping.

Keeping an eye on the world going by my window,
Takin' my time.

When I wake up early in the morning,
Lift my head, I'm still yawning,
When I'm in the middle of a dream,
Stay in bed, float upstream.

Please don't wake me,
No, don't shake me,
Leave me where I am;
I'm only sleeping.

Rip Van Winkle

A long time ago, a man named Rip Van Winkle lived in a small village beneath the Catskill Mountains in New York State. Rip spent a lot of his time in the mountains. Unfortunately, it wasn't because he was an adventurer or hiker. It was because he wanted to escape from his wife. All day long, she would nag him about what work he should do on his farm, and sometimes she followed her yells with a well-aimed shoe!

It was true that Rip was not a very hard worker, but he was a nice man who was always kind to children and animals. The things he most liked to do were talk with his friends in the village and stroll through the woods. They were the only escapes he had from his sharp-tongued wife and all the work to be done.

One afternoon in autumn, Rip was walking through a valley in the mountains. The trees had never looked prettier, and Rip stopped often to admire a leaf or gaze up into the distant mountain peaks.

As he walked along, he heard a loud sound coming from the top of a mountain. "I wonder what that could be?" he asked himself and started toward the noise. The way up the slope was difficult, and by the time he reached the peak, Rip was sweaty and thirsty. He pushed his way into a clearing. Rip suddenly caught his breath, for there before him was a whole group of little men, all dressed strangely, all no taller then his waist, all with faces as green as sour apples! And what was even stranger, they appeared to be playing a noisy bowling game called

ninepins! At the sight of Rip, they all stopped and stared at him. Slowly, a little man wearing an especially big hat stepped forward.

"Good evening, Rip," he said solemnly. Before Rip could wonder how he knew his name, the little man continued. "Will you open a barrel for us? We are all thirsty from our game." He motioned toward a large barrel at the side of the clearing.

Rip was nervous but didn't see any harm in helping out the little men. He went to the barrel and pried it open. The barrel was full of rich, creamy apple cider and the scent was so sweet that Rip felt dizzy just smelling it. The little man dipped a mug in, took a deep drink, and resumed his game with the others.

Rip watched the game for a while, wondering at the strangeness of these events, but soon realized how thirsty he was.

"Surely these men won't mind it I take a small sip?" he thought as he scooped some into his mouth. The cider was sweet and thick and good. Rip took another drink and licked his lips.

Suddenly Rip began to yawn. His eyelids felt like lead, and he found that he could barely keep his head up.

"Maybe I'd better take a short nap under that tree," he murmured, stumbling over to a leafy oak tree and lying down. In two seconds, he was snoring deeply.

When Rip woke up, he noticed that all the men were gone and it was practically night. "Oh no," he groaned, thinking of the scolding his wife was going to give him. He stood up slowly and noticed his joints were a lot creakier than they had been before.

"Sleeping outside certainly makes your bones stiff," he thought. Rip spent a few minutes stretching and loosening up his body. Then he slowly made his way down the mountain toward home.

From the moment he walked up the main road, he could feel people looking at him strangely. And he looked at them strangely too, for he didn't recognize a single person he saw!

When he got to his house, all he found was an old abandoned cottage with a caved-in roof and broken windows. It was obvious that no one had lived there for a while.

Bewildered, he wandered back to the village square and stopped a man walking past. "What happened to the old general store?" he asked. The man answered, "The general store? That was torn down ten years ago to make room for the new meeting hall."

"Well, where is Nicholas Vedder, who owned the store?"

The man looked at him strangely, "Nicholas Vedder joined the army."

"And Van Bummel, the schoolmaster?"

"He became a great general and now he's in Congress."

Rip suddenly felt weak. Bringing his hand to his chest, he felt a long beard trailing from his chin. He whispered, "And Rip Van Winkle? Do you remember him?"

"Rip Van Winkle? Yeah, he went up to the mountains twenty years ago and never came back."

Twenty years ago! "But I am Rip Van Winkle!" he gasped.

By this time, a crowd had gathered around the strange man who claimed to be the missing Rip. A young woman pushed herself to the front of the crowd. "You say you are Rip Van Winkle?" she asked, "Well, then you'll have no trouble remembering the name of your little daughter's favorite doll."

Although in a fog, Rip muttered, "Why, it's Betty. The doll was Betty."

The woman gasped, for she was Rip Van Winkle's daughter, now grown up, with children of her own. She embraced her father and led him to her house, where he was amazed to meet his grandchildren.

After that day, Rip stayed with his daughter and helped the family around the house. Although it took him a while to get used to the town's changes, he became happy with his new life. He was sorry to hear many of his friends were gone, but he was secretly relieved that his wife, who had passed away after throwing a very violent fit, was no longer around to yell at him. Now he could talk to people all he wanted. Rip spent his days sitting in the village square, telling everyone the amazing story of his trip into the Catskills and his meeting with the little green men. Not everyone believed his tale, but there were more than a few people in the village who, when faced with an angry wife, husband, or parent, wished for just a small sip of that magical, sleepy cider Rip had drank up. ✦

A GOOD

Children need at least nine hours of sleep per night to feel rested and ready for the day ahead of them. With simple planning and a consistent schedule, it's easy to get the required shut-eye.

Resistance to bedtime, nightmares, and the inability to fall asleep are all problems that can interfere with a good night's rest. Here are some general guidelines to put you on the right path.

Falling Asleep

Make sure your bed is comfortable and the room is dark and quiet enough to fall asleep in. You might need a night-light or a door to be slightly ajar. A small amount of light might be just enough to make you feel safe in your room. Just make sure it doesn't distract you from going to sleep.

Try not to use your bed for lots of activities other than sleep. That way, getting ready for bed sends a signal to your brain that it's time to go to sleep.

Go to bed and get up at the same time every day. It's important to stick to a sleep schedule. Your body likes routine.

Try not to be very active close to bedtime.

Do something quiet, such as take a bath, read a bedtime story, or play quietly with some toys. This will prepare your body for sleep.

Don't drink soda or caffeinated beverages. The caffeine can keep you awake, even if you drank it seven hours before your bedtime!

Try not to eat a big meal right before you go to sleep. Sometimes you might want to have a little snack so you won't feel hungry, but don't eat too much. Try the helpful recipes in this book for a list of foods that are good for a sleepy tummy.

If you find yourself tossing and turning, try one of the helpful relaxation exercises on page 154.

Try sleeping with a stuffed animal or blanket. Sometimes it's reassuring to have a familiar object with you when you go to sleep.

If you have the same nightmare over and over, try re-imagining the ending during the day. Thinking of a happy ending can sometimes make the nightmare go away.

Avoid scary movies and scary books right before bedtime.

Think about anything that might be

SLEEP

bothering you during the day. If you have a problem or are worried about something, talk to your parents or an adult you know you can trust, such as a favorite teacher. Sometimes you can stop being scared of something just by talking about it.

Tips for Mom

To calm sincere nighttime fears, agree to sit quietly in the dark in a chair in the corner— or lie on the floor, if that's comfortable for you—for ten or fifteen minutes. Don't agree to requests for more stories or conversation. Greet attempts to interact with you with a soothing "Shhh, it's time for sleep." Try not to stay until your child is asleep. Your child will expect you to be there if he or she awakes in the middle of the night, or you will find yourself in their room every evening, waiting until they fall asleep. It's better to leave and respond to their calls than to begin the habit of waiting until they fall asleep.

It's not uncommon for children to suddenly remember something they have to tell you five minutes after the lights go out. And then five minutes after that, they need a drink of water. And five minutes after that, they insist they can't possibly fall asleep. Nip this behavior in the bud, or "bedtime" can extend into a seeming eternity. And it's hard to break the habit once it's gotten a good hold.

When your child just can't settle down, try softly stroking their face from forehead down the nose to the chin. Your child's eyes will reflexively close as you repeat this motion.

Brahms' Lullaby

Lullaby, and good night,
In the sky stars are bright;
Round your head, flowers gay
Scent your slumbers till day.

Close your eyes now and rest,
May these hours be blest,
Go to sleep now and rest,
May these hours be blest.

SOOTHING

EARLY DINNERS CAN LEAVE LITTLE TUMMIES RUMBLING by bedtime. Keep Peanut Butter and Banana Squares or some ingredients for sandwiches or smoothies available for a quick snack. Each of the recipes below contains complex carbohydrates and protein *(see page 42)*, as well as calcium (another snooze promoter). Tuna fish and whole wheat bread, eggs and pita, hummus, turkey, and beans are all powerful sleep helpers. And instead of a sugary dessert, try a frosty smoothie.

Peanut Butter and Banana Squares
2 cups uncooked oats
1/3 cup peanut butter
2 bananas, peeled and sliced

1. Preheat the oven to 350°F.
2. Combine the oats and peanut butter in a bowl. Mix thoroughly.
3. Spread the mixture into a greased 8-inch-square baking pan.
4. Bake for 25 minutes. Let cool.
5. Cut into squares and top each with a slice of banana.

Makes 24 squares.

Hummus and Pita Pockets
Hummus:
1 (15-ounce) can chickpeas
8 ounces plain yogurt
1/4 cup lemon juice

SNACKS

1/4 cup tahini paste
1 clove garlic, crushed
1 tablespoon fresh parsley
2 tablespoons olive oil
salt to taste

Combine all ingredients in a blender and whip until smooth.

Makes 2 cups.

Pita Pockets:
2 pitas
1/2 small cucumber, peeled and sliced

1. Cut each pita in half.
2. Fill each pita pocket with hummus and add some cucumber slices.

Makes 4 pockets.

Tuna Fish Stars
2 slices whole wheat bread
1 (6-ounce) can tuna in water, drained
2 tablespoons mayonnaise
shredded lettuce
1 tomato, sliced

1. Stack the two bread slices. Using a large star-shaped cookie cutter, cut out the shape.
2. Combine the tuna and mayonnaise in a bowl and mix thoroughly.

3. Spread the tuna salad on one piece of star-shaped bread. Add lettuce and tomato slices. Top it off with the other slice of bread.

Makes 1 serving.

Egg Salad in a Pita
2 tablespoons mayonnaise
3 hard-boiled eggs, chopped
1/2 stalk celery, chopped
1/4 green pepper, chopped
salt and pepper to taste
3 whole wheat pitas

1. Combine all ingredients except pitas in a bowl. Mix thoroughly.
2. Spoon egg salad into pitas.

Makes 3 servings.

Turkey Roll-Up
2 slices turkey
mayonnaise
shredded lettuce
soft tortilla

1. Spread mayonnaise on the tortilla.
2. Layer the turkey and lettuce.
3. Roll up and cut in half.

Makes 2 small roll ups.

SOOTHING SNACKS

Beans & Rice Burrito

3/4 cup uncooked white rice
2 cups water
1 (15-ounce) can black beans
2 tablespoons lemon juice
1 tablespoon garlic powder
1 1/2 teaspoon cilantro
3 tortillas
1/2 cup cheddar cheese, shredded (optional)

1. In a medium-size pot, bring the water to a boil. Add rice.
2. Reduce heat, cover, and let rice simmer for about 15 minutes or until tender and water is absorbed (test a grain to see if it's soft without being mushy).
3. Add the beans to the rice and continue to heat over a medium flame, stirring frequently, until slowly bubbling. Remove from heat.
4. Stir in lemon juice, garlic powder, and cilantro.
5. Cool slightly, and then divide mixture among 3 tortillas, fold in sides, and roll up. Or serve in bowls with a light sprinkling of shredded cheddar cheese on top.

Makes 3 servings.

Sleepy Smoothies

Bananas, yogurt, and milk are perfect good-night foods, but you don't have to eat them plain. Try one of these fresh and fabulous smoothies to help you get to sleep. Combine all ingredients for each recipe in a blender, and blend until smooth. Pour into glasses and serve. Each recipe makes 2 servings.

Fruit Fantasy: *7 big strawberries (remove the leafy stems), 1 banana (broken up), 2 peaches, 1 cup orange or orange-combination juice, 2 cups ice*

A Tropical Dream: *7 big frozen strawberries, 1 (8-ounce) container lemon yogurt, 1/3 cup orange or other fruit juice*

Peanut Butter Paradise: *1 banana (broken up), 3 tablespoons peanut butter, 1/2 cup milk (soy, whole, or skim), 2 tablespoons honey*

Chocolate Banana: *3/4 cup chocolate milk, 1/2 cup chocolate sorbet, 1 1/4 cup frozen raspberries, 1/2 banana (broken up), sprinkling of nutmeg*

It's too late to tell stories now," the Old-Green-Grasshopper announced. "it's time to go to sleep."

"I refuse to sleep in my boots!" the Centipede cried. "How many more are there to come off, James?"

"I think I've done about twenty so far," James told him.

"Then that leaves eighty to go," the Centipede said.

"*Twenty-two*, not *eighty*!" shrieked the Earthworm. "He's lying again."

The Centipede roared with laughter.

"Stop pulling the Earthworm's leg," the Ladybug said.

This sent the Centipede into hysterics. "Pulling his *leg*!" he cried, wriggling with glee and pointing at the Earthworm. "Which leg am I pulling? You tell me that?"

James decided that he rather liked the Centipede. He was obviously a rascal, but what a change it was to hear somebody laughing once in a while. He had never heard Aunt Sponge or Aunt Spiker laughing aloud in all the time he had been with them.

"We really *must* get some sleep," the Old-Green-Grasshopper said. "We've got a tough day ahead of us tomorrow. So would you be kind enough, Miss Spider, to make the beds?"

James and the Giant Peach

Roald Dahl

A few minutes later, Miss Spider had made the first bed. It was hanging from the ceiling, suspended by a rope of threads at either end so that actually it looked more like a hammock than a bed. But it was a magnificent affair, and the stuff that it was made of shimmered like silk in the pale light.

"I do hope you'll find it comfortable," Miss Spider said to the Old-Green-Grasshopper. "I made it as soft and silky as I possibly could. I spun it with gossamer. That's a much better quality thread than the one I use for my own web."

"Thank you so much, my dear lady," the Old-Green-Grasshopper said, climbing into the hammock. "Ah, this is just what I needed. Good night, everybody. Good night."

Then Miss Spider spun the next hammock, and the Ladybug got in.

After that, she spun a long one for the Centipede, and an even longer one for the Earthworm.

"And how do you like *your* bed?" she said to James when it came to his turn. "Hard or soft?"

"I like it soft, thank you very much," James answered.

"For goodness' sake stop staring around the room and get on with my boots!" the Centipede said. "You and I are never going to get any sleep at this rate! And kindly line them up neatly in pairs as you take them off. Don't just throw them over your shoulder."

James worked away frantically on the Centipede's boots. Each one had laces that had to be untied and loosened before it could be pulled off, and to make matters worse, all the laces were tied up in the most complicated knots that had to be unpicked with fingernails. It was just awful. It took about two hours. And by the time James had pulled off the last boot of all and had lined them up in a row on the floor—twenty-one pairs altogether—the Centipede was fast asleep.

"Wake up, Centipede," whispered James, giving him a gentle dig in the stomach. "It's time for bed."

"Thank you, my dear child," the Centipede said, opening his eyes. Then he got down off the sofa and ambled across the room and crawled into his hammock. James got into his own hammock—and oh, how soft and comfortable it was compared with the hard bare boards that his aunts had always made him sleep upon at home.

"Lights out," said the Centipede drowsily.

Nothing happened.

"Turn out the light!" he called, raising his voice.

James glanced round the room, wondering which of the others he might be talking to, but they were all asleep. The Old-Green-Grasshopper was snoring loudly through his nose. The Ladybug was making whistling noises as she breathed, and the Earthworm was coiled up like a spring at one end of his hammock, wheezing and blowing through his open mouth. As for Miss Spider, she had made a lovely web for herself across one corner of the room, and James could see her crouching right in the very center of it, mumbling softly in her dreams.

"I said turn out the light!" shouted the Centipede angrily.

"Are you talking to me?" James asked him.

"Of course I'm not talking to you, you ass!" the Centipede answered. "That crazy Glow-worm has gone to sleep with her light on!"

For the first time since entering the room, James glanced up at the ceiling—and there he saw a most extraordinary sight. Something that looked like a gigantic fly without wings (it was at least three feet long) was standing upside down upon its six legs in the middle of the ceiling, and the tail end of this creature seemed to be literally on fire. A brilliant greenish light as bright as the brightest electric bulb was shining out of its tail and lighting up the whole room.

"Is *that* a Glow-worm?" asked James, staring at the light. "It doesn't look like a worm of any sort to me."

"Of course it's a Glow-worm," the Centipede answered. "At least that's what *she* calls herself. Although actually you are quite right. She isn't really a worm at all. Glow-worms are never worms. They are simply lady fireflies without wings. Wake up, you lazy beast!" But the Glow-worm didn't stir, so the Centipede reached out of his hammock and picked up one of his boots from the floor. "Put out that wretched light!" he shouted, hurling the boot up at the ceiling.

The Glow-worm slowly opened one eye and stared at the Centipede. "There is no need to be rude," she said coldly. "All in good time."

"Come on, come on, come on!" shouted the Centipede, "Or I'll put it out for you!"

"Oh, hello, James!" the Glow-worm said, looking down and giving James a little wave and a smile. "I didn't see you come in. Welcome, my dear boy, welcome—and good night!"

Then *click*—and out went the light.

James Henry Trotter lay there in the darkness with his eyes wide open, listening to the strange sleeping noises that the "creatures" were making all around him, and wondering what on earth was going to happen to him in the morning. Already, he was beginning to like his new friends very much. They were not nearly as terrible as they looked. In fact, they weren't really terrible at all. They seemed extremely kind and helpful in spite of all the shouting and arguing that went on between them.

"Good night, Old-Green-Grasshopper," he whispered. "Good night, Ladybug—Good night, Miss Spider—" But before he could go through them all, he had fallen fast asleep. ☾

TWINKLING

Many animals, plants, and insects only come out at night, but few are easier to observe than the lovely firefly. Also known as lightning bugs, fireflies glitter in the evening in dark areas during warm–weather months. When this member of the beetle family breathes in oxygen, the oxygen combines with luciferin, a substance in the insect's body, causing a chemical reaction that produces the luminous glow. Fireflies use this light to attract mates and prey, and to tell predators to keep away! Use your new knowledge of these "brilliant" creatures to observe them the next clear, warm night.

Catch a Firefly

Flashlight, butterfly net, jar or plastic container with holes poked in lid.

1. Fireflies are attracted to warm, moist places, especially areas around swamps, ponds, and forests. However, fireflies have also been found in very dry places, too.

FIREFLIES

In North America, fireflies are predominantly found up and down the East Coast and as far west as Kansas. Different species of fireflies like to make their entrance at different times in the night, but most like to come out at dusk, the warmest part of the evening. They usually appear in early summer and stay until fall begins.

2. Look for fireflies in dark and quiet places, away from brightly lit houses or busy streets. Turn off any extra lights to make sure to attract some lightning bugs.

3. Look for the telltale green light of the firefly. If it's moving around (meaning that the fly is probably male), study the pattern of the light and try to imitate it with a flashlight. He will fly up to you, thinking you are a female firefly answering his light signal.

4. Try to catch the firefly with cupped hands or a butterfly net.

5. If you manage to catch one, place it carefully in the plastic container. Set it free before you go to bed, since fireflies do not survive long in captivity.

Firefly Facts

★ There are over 1100 species of firefly throughout the world. North America is home to about 170 species.

★ Firefly larvae feed on slugs, worms, and snails. They use their mandibles to inject their prey with a fluid that paralyzes them until they can be eaten.

★ Some Asian firefly larvae are born underwater, and feast on aquatic snails before becoming adults.

★ That glow may be pretty, but it could also spell danger. Especially if you're a firefly from a different species! Some fireflies use their lights to mimic the flashes of other firefly species. Then when the other species is tricked into thinking it has found a mate, the first firefly eats it.

★ In some areas, fireflies light up in synch with each other! Following a single bug, they will flash their lights in glowing waves.

★ The part of the firefly's body that gives off light makes up one half of its total body weight.

$\mathcal{M}$ay every creature
abound in well-being and peace.

May every living being,
weak or strong, the long and the small,
the short and medium-sized,
the mean and the great,

May every living creature,
seen and unseen
those dwelling far off,
those wanting to be born,

May all attain peace.

—*Buddhist*

Pecos Bill

Whenever folks out West gather around a big blazing fire and watch the stars twinkle and shine above, they can hear the howl of the wolves out on the prairie. It's a high, lonesome sound, and most folks wonder what it is the wolves have to be so sad about—what it is that makes them sound so awfully lonely. The answer can't be found in a story about the wolves, but rather in the legend of the most famous, wildest, best cowboy of all: Pecos Bill.

Pecos Bill was born on a wagon train heading out West. He had ten brothers and sisters. One day, when Pecos was still a baby, his mother put him down for a nap under a shady tree. Before she knew it, a giant bear lumbered out of the nearby woods and chased her and the family away. With all those kids to account for, nobody noticed Pecos was missing until they were already two states away!

Now, Pecos Bill might have ended up in a lot of trouble, but luckily, a wolf pack was passing through the area. They found the baby and decided to adopt little Pecos as their own. He grew up playing with his wolf brothers, learning everything there was to know about the land, and just having a grand old time. People say he got his wildness from this strange upbringing.

As Pecos Bill got older, his reputation got bigger and spread through the whole country. It was said he once roped a tornado and rode it all over the land just for fun. He was the only cowboy to tame the craziest, most furious horse, Widowmaker, and of course they became best friends afterward.

But the story that explains why the wolves howl so mournfully at the moon each night is actually the story of how Pecos fell in love. One day, while he was riding Widowmaker by the Rio Grande, he spied a beautiful girl. And she wasn't swimming or sunbathing; she was riding the biggest catfish Pecos had ever seen! Right there, Pecos Bill knew this was the only girl he'd ever love. When she came ashore, he asked her two questions: What was her name, and would she have his hand in marriage?

The girl smiled and proudly told him her name was Slue-Foot Sue, the wildest and toughest cowgirl in the West. But when she came to the marriage proposal, she blushed and looked at the ground. After Sue realized who was asking for her hand in marriage, she knew there was no one in the West who was wilder or better than Pecos Bill was. So she accepted. Pecos was so happy, he jumped across the Rio Grande four times!

But Slue-Foot Sue had two conditions. "Anything, anything at all!" Pecos agreed, rather foolishly in this case. One was that her wedding dress would include a new-fangled fashion accessory called a bustle. This wire contraption was attached to a lady's petticoat on her behind and made the back of her skirt flare out. Although Pecos thought it was a very silly thing, he knew how important the day would be to Slue-Foot Sue, so he agreed.

Sue gave him her best smile. "And two, I want to ride Widowmaker to the church." Slue-Foot Sue had heard the many stories about Pecos Bill's famous horse, and she wanted to prove she was just as good a cowboy as Pecos was.

Pecos Bill turned as white as a ghost. "But I'm the only one who can ride Widowmaker," he whispered. Slue-Foot Sue turned away. "Then I guess the wedding is off." Finally, Pecos agreed to let her ride his horse. He was just too head over heels in love to say no.

The day of the wedding, Pecos had a long talk with Widowmaker and tried to get him to behave when Sue stepped up for her ride. Even so, that horse was angry! His eyes were red and he kicked his legs out at anyone near him. It took seven strong men just to lead him to the street

that went up to the church!

Slue-Foot Sue didn't mind. She felt very fine in her beautiful wedding dress with her "sophisticated" bustle attached to her skirt. Daintily, she stepped up to the furious horse. Calmly, she put one leg over his side.

And that's as far as she got before Widowmaker shot off, bucking and trying desperately to shake Sue loose. Everyone gathered round, hoping that Sue wouldn't hurt herself when she fell off, but Sue was an excellent cowgirl, and she held on for dear life.

All of a sudden, Widowmaker gave the biggest buck ever, and Sue shot straight into the clouds! She went up like a rocket, at least a mile into the sky! Everyone rushed around trying to find something to catch her with. Pecos wrung his hat and yelled, "Get a net! A cushion! Something! We've got to catch her!"

But before anyone could do a thing, Slue-Foot Sue came plummeting back toward earth, down, down, down, at least fifty miles an hour, and then she BOUNCED straight up in the air again! She had landed right on her bustle, and the wire contraption acted just like a spring! Sue kept going up, higher and higher, then falling down and down, only to land on her bouncy bustle and shoot straight back up in the sky again! She bounced up and down for a week, and Pecos tried to lasso her many times, but he just couldn't do it.

Finally, one night, Slue-Foot Sue bounced so hard and so high that she ended up reaching the moon. And that's where she stayed. Heartbroken, Pecos Bill went to live with his wolf family for a while. Every night he would stare at the big, silvery moon and imagine his true love up there. Then he would open his mouth wide and howl out a hello. But she never answered back, so his howls got sadder and sadder, and soon the whole wolf family was joining him.

So, when you hear the wolves howling at the moon on lonely nights, it's because they're remembering their good friend Pecos Bill, and his true love.

All the Pretty Little Horses

Hush-a-bye,
Don't you cry.
Go to sleep-y
little baby,
Blacks and bays,
Dapples and grays,
Coach and
six-a-little horses.

Hush-a-bye,
Don't you cry.
Go to sleep-y
little baby,

When you wake,
you shall have
all the pretty
little horses.
Blacks and bays,
Dapples and grays,
coach and
six-a-little horses.

Hush-a-bye,
Don't you cry.
Go to sleep-y
little baby.

Night Creature

I like
the quiet breathing
of the night,

the tree talk
the wind-swish
the star light.

Day is
glare-y
loud
scary.
Day bustles.

Night rustles.
I like
night.

—*Lilian Moore*

SHADOW

What animals only come out in the dark? Shadow puppet animals! To glimpse them, all you need is a lamp, a bare wall, and your hands.

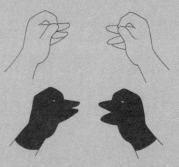

Pull your right thumb away from your fingers to make a panther roar.

Move your right thumb for a boxing wallaby.

Wiggle your fingers to make the spider walk.

Shift your fourth finger and pinky to make the birds talk.

PUPPETS

Try moving your hands so that your dog sniffs the air.

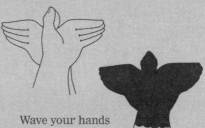

Twitch your rabbit's ears by moving the third and fourth fingers of your left hand.

paper plate

Wave your hands to make the bird fly.

Pull back your right arm to make the snail disappear into its shell.

The Rabbit in the Moon

Long ago, the great philosopher Buddha was wandering through a forest. He was so busy enjoying the cool shadows, leafy trees, and soft sounds all around him that he soon lost sight of the path. This did not bother him, as he could easily find it again, and he walked on until sunset. Just as he was about to turn back, he found a neat little cottage with a thatched roof sitting in the middle of a tiny clearing. He realized this was the home of Rabbit, Monkey, and Fox, who were all friends. They had decided to live in the woods together, and they all got along very nicely. In the morning, Monkey would climb the trees to gather fruit for breakfast, and in the evening, Fox would go fishing to catch his friends some supper. Rabbit was content to tidy up their little house, since he nibbled only on grass and roots anyway.

Buddha saw the charming little house and the animals sitting contently outside around a large campfire. Though the three friends were very good to each other, Buddha was curious to see how generous they would be to a stranger. He quickly disguised himself as an old, tired man to test them.

He stumbled up to them. "I'm sorry to bother you," he said, "but I've lost my way, and now I don't know how to get back home. Could I perhaps trouble you for a bite to eat? I'm very hungry and I've been walking all day long."

Monkey looked at the old man and noticed his bare, dirty feet. "Certainly," said Monkey, and he grabbed some old bananas that had been sitting in the house and placed them in front of the man.

"I can do better than that," cried Fox, after noticing the big holes in the man's clothes. He took the half-eaten portion of the fish he had caught that day and gave it to the man.

Now, Rabbit began to feel embarrassed. Although the man was ragged, unlike Fox or Monkey he didn't see his tattered clothes or dirty face. He saw only a man who was lost, cold, and hungry. He deserved a good meal. Unfortunately, Rabbit had nothing to offer the old man. "I usually don't eat bananas or fish," he began, "the only things I nibble on are grass and roots, and I don't think you'd be too interested in that." Rabbit looked around, but he could not think of a single thing to give the man to eat.

Finally, he said, "If you are still hungry, I guess you can go ahead and eat me."

Monkey and Fox were astonished! How could Rabbit offer up his very life to this old man? He was probably a beggar, anyway, and used to being hungry. It was fine to offer some old bananas or half-eaten fish, but Rabbit was really going too far!

Rabbit advised Monkey and Fox to build the fire up high. He would jump directly into it and cook himself. He said good-bye to his friends, shut his eyes, and then took a giant leap at the fire. But to his surprise, he just hung in midair. He cracked open an eye and realized the old man had caught him by his long ears and was now laughing.

Suddenly, Buddha shrugged off his disguise, and all the animals gasped. Buddha gently put Rabbit down.

"I'm sorry to play such tricks on you," he told the animals, "but I was passing through the forest and couldn't resist testing to see which of you was the most generous animal. The food Fox and Monkey offered me was satisfactory, but not something they would offer to a guest." Fox and Monkey hung their heads and felt bad about offering Buddha only old or half-eaten things. "But Rabbit provided the greatest sacrifice of all by offering up himself so an old man could be fed."

Buddha clapped his hands. "For your offering, Rabbit, I will reward you by bringing you to the moon with me, where you can look down on all the world. And all the world can look up at you and remember what it is to be so unselfish."

He gathered Rabbit up in his arms, and after waving good-bye to Fox and Monkey, sailed up into the stars, carrying the little rabbit with him.

And to this day, many people think the dark spots on the moon's face are actually shadows cast by Rabbit—now an old bunny—and his many, many children.

MOON RIVER

By Henry Mancini and Johnny Mercer

Moon River, wider than a mile,
I'm crossin' you in style some day.
Old dream maker, you heart breaker,
wherever you're goin' I'm goin' your way.
Two drifters, off to see the world.
There's such a lot of world to see.
We're after the same rainbow's end—
waitin' 'round the bend,
my Huckleberry friend,
Moon River and me.

Is the Moon Tired?

Is the moon tired? She looks so pale
Within her misty veil;
She scales the sky from east to west,
And takes no rest.

Before the coming of the night
The moon shows papery white;
Before the dawning of the day
She fades away.

—Christina Rossetti

GOOD NIGHT

By John Lennon and Paul McCartney

Now it's time to say good night;
Good night, sleep tight.
Now the sun turns out his light;
Good night, sleep tight.
Dream sweet dreams for me.
Dream sweet dreams for you.

Close your eyes and I'll close mine.
Good night, sleep tight.
Now the moon begins to shine,
Good night, sleep tight.
Dream sweet dreams for me,
Dream sweet dreams for you.

Close your eyes and I'll close mine.
Good night, sleep tight.
Now the sun turns out his light,
Good night, sleep tight.
Dream sweet dreams for me,
Dream sweet dreams for you.

Good night, ev'rybody,
Ev'rybody, ev'rywhere,
Good night.

The Nightingale

Once upon a time, there was an emperor who lived in the most beautiful castle in the world. It was filled with fantastic things and wonderful toys. His garden was full of gorgeous flowers, blue ponds, and tall trees. He made it even more wonderful by having little silver bells tied to the flower stems. That way, every time a breeze whispered through, all the little flowers would shake and make the prettiest sounds.

People from all over the world traveled to the emperor's city, and the emperor loved hearing them talk about his treasures. One day, he was listening to a visitor admire the wonders of his garden: the sweet flowers, the cool ponds, and the beautiful music of the small bird, the nightingale. "Nightingale?" The emperor interrupted. "What nightingale? In my garden? I've never even heard it." He was so curious about the nightingale that he summoned all the court and asked every single one of the high-and-mighty nobles about the nightingale. No one knew what he was talking about. Finally, a little girl who swept the floor in the grand kitchen stepped forward. She was very nervous to be talking to the emperor, but she said, "I know where the nightingale is. Whenever I walk alone at night through the gardens to get to my house, I always hear her sing. Her songs are so beautiful that even if I've worked the whole day, I still feel like dancing!"

The emperor asked the girl to lead him and his entire court to the famous nightingale. As they were walking through the garden, one noble tried to impress the emperor, saying, "Oh, I

hear the nightingale!" But the little kitchen girl said, "No, that is just a frog croaking." Then a silly lady said, "What is that pretty sound? It must be the nightingale!" But the little kitchen girl tried to hide her smile and said, "No, that is just a cow mooing."

At last, they came to the nightingale's tree. She was singing so beautifully that everyone was speechless, including the emperor. When she finished her song, the emperor stepped forward and said, "Little nightingale, your song is the loveliest I have ever heard. Will you come to my palace and sing me to sleep every night?"

"My song sounds best in the green woods," the nightingale replied, but she agreed to fly to the emperor's bedroom every evening so she could sing him a sweet good-night song. The nightingale became so famous after that, people would gather outside the emperor's window to hear her song every night. The townspeople named children after her, and some ladies would try to imitate her singing voice.

One day, the emperor received a mysterious package. All it said on it was "The Nightingale." When he opened it up, he was amazed to find a little nightingale toy made out of gold and jewels. Following the instructions, he wound the toy up and listened to it play the most beautiful song ever. The little tail moved up and down and its diamond eyes sparkled. Everyone loved the new nightingale, but when the real nightingale saw it, she sighed and flew away. She knew the emperor would not want her around now that he had this new toy to sing him to sleep. When the emperor found out she was gone, he got very angry and said she was not allowed in the palace ever again.

A year passed and the emperor listened to the new nightingale every night. Even though the toy was getting worn down, he couldn't sleep without it. Then something very bad happened. The emperor became sick and had to stay in bed all the time. Every day he became weaker and weaker, and people were afraid to talk above a whisper. The whole castle became very, very quiet so the emperor would not be disturbed.

But the reason the emperor was so sick was that he could not sleep! You see, the little toy bird had finally broken, and now it sat in the corner, silent and forgotten. Without the soothing music it made, the emperor tossed and turned all night until the sun came up. One day, he no longer had the strength to pick his head up. All of the servants started looking for new jobs; they didn't think he could live much longer.

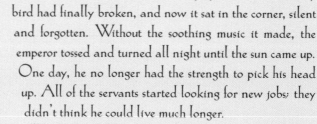

"If only I could hear the real nightingale," the emperor said to himself. "I'm sure I could sleep if I heard just one of her songs." Suddenly, he heard a wonderful sound coming from his window. He moved his eyes and saw the real nightingale sitting on the ledge, singing her beautiful song. He wanted to tell her how much he loved her, but he was too weak. Instead, he listened to the music and fell into a deep, refreshing sleep.

The next day, he felt much, much better after having a good night's rest. "I can't believe I wanted to replace you with this toy." He told the nightingale, picking up the fake nightingale and throwing it in the garbage.

"No, don't do that," she said. "The toy did what it could. It couldn't help being broken." The emperor wiggled his toes and smiled. He felt so strong after his beautiful rest that he was ready to run all around the palace. "I will give you riches and gold. You will have a bed made out of silk right here by my head!"

The nightingale shook her wings. "I cannot live here in the palace with you. But let me come every night to sing you a bedtime song, and we will both be happy."

So every night, the emperor would curl up in his big, soft bed, and the little nightingale would sit on his window and sing the sweetest songs to him. He would close his eyes and soon be asleep, drifting away on the beautiful melodies.

O heavenly Father, protect and bless
all things that have breath;
guard them from all evil
and let them sleep in peace.

—*Albert Schweitzer*

May the sun rise well;
may the earth appear
brightly shone upon!

May the moon rise well;
may the earth appear
brightly shone upon!

—*Teton Sioux*

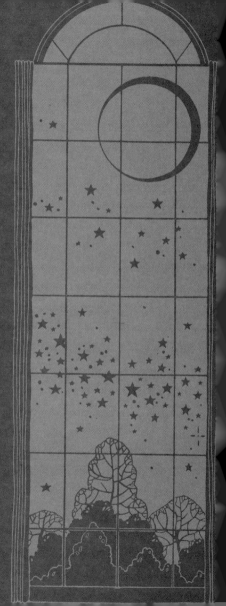

Peter Pan

J. M. Barrie

Mrs. Darling first heard of Peter when she was tidying up her children's minds. It is the nightly custom of every good mother after her children are asleep to rummage in their minds and put things straight for next morning, repacking into their proper places the many articles that have wandered during the day. If you could keep awake (but of course you can't) you would see your own mother doing this, and you would find it very interesting to watch her. It is quite like tidying up drawers. You would see her on her knees, I expect, lingering humorously over some of your contents, wondering where on earth you had picked this thing up, making discoveries sweet and not so sweet, pressing this to her cheek as if it were as nice as a kitten, and hurriedly stowing that out of sight. When you wake in the morning, the naughtiness and evil passions with which you went to bed have been folded up small and placed at the bottom of your mind; and on the top, beautifully aired, are spread out your prettier thoughts, ready for you to put on. ☾

DREAMS

Dreams have always been important to human beings. In many ancient cultures, people believed that dreams were messages sent to them by gods or warnings about dangers to come. Although some people still think dreams can predict the future, many people believe dreams are actually made up of things that you have seen, heard, smelled, tasted, or done during the day. These things are called stimuli. You might not know it, but your brain is so amazing that it will remember a lot of stimuli that you were barely paying attention to when you were awake. Then, once you are asleep, your brain sorts through this stimuli. Dreams are like your brain giving your head a good spring cleaning every night! Sometimes the stimuli get all jumbled up, which is why some of your dreams seem confusing or even frightening. By trying to figure out what your dreams mean, you can see what your brain is trying to tell you while you are asleep.

Dream Journal
Notebook, pen or pencil

1. The first step to understanding your dreams is remembering them. Keeping a journal will help you recall your dreams.
2. Keep your notebook and pen within easy reach. Under your pillow is a good spot.
3. When you wake up in the morning, keep your eyes closed for a while and stay in bed.
4. Try to remember what you dreamed about. One moment, scene, or action can be all you need to start remembering more.
5. Use the notebook and pen to write or draw a picture of what you remember. You don't have to remember everything, just record what you can think of. As the day goes on, you might remember more things to add.
6. Don't be frustrated if you can't remember your dreams at first. It takes practice. You might be surprised at how many details you can come up with!

DREAMS

Dream Symbolism

Pay attention to things you see, hear, feel, and do in your dreams. These are called symbols. Some kinds of symbols occur frequently in dreams. Here are some common symbols and what people think they mean.

Animals

★ Beaver: Through hard work, you will get what you wish for.

★ Fish: Good luck is headed your way. This is especially good if you dream of a goldfish.

★ Puppy: You're going to meet or have met someone who will be a good friend.

★ Rabbits: Something very good is about to happen to you.

Colors

★ Pink: Love and healing through love

★ Red: Passion, anger, or strong emotion

★ Gray: Fear and confusion

★ White: Truth and new beginnings

★ Green: Healing and growth

★ Yellow: Peace, hope, and happiness

Objects

★ Angels: You will find peace and joy.

★ Baby: Good fortune and helpful friends

★ Bus or Train: You are moving on and heading toward a goal.

★ Dancing: Fun times are coming up!

★ Telephone: If it's ringing, your mind is trying to tell you something.

Food

★ Birthday cake: Many of your wishes will come true.

★ Candy: Rewards are heading your way.

★ Eggs: Something new is about to happen.

★ Tea: You are happy with your life and taking the time to enjoy it!

Places

★ Airport: There may be an idea or plan you are working on that is about to take off.

★ Beach: You are looking forward to some relaxation or a break from the ordinary. Could summer vacation be far ahead?

★ Fork in the road: You are facing an important decision in your life.

★ Forest: Trees that are tall and green mean you are about to grow in some way.

★ Mountains: In order to realize your goals, you'll be faced with many challenges.

★ School: You are learning an important lesson.

DREAM A LITTLE DREAM OF ME

By Gus Kahn

Stars shining bright above you,
Night breezes seem to whisper, "I love you,"
Birds singing in the sycamore tree,
"Dream a little dream of me."

Say "Night-ie night" and kiss me,
Just hold me tight and tell me you'll miss me;
While I'm alone and blue as can be,
Dream a little dream of me

Stars fading, but I linger on, dear,
Still craving your kiss;
I'm longing to linger till dawn, dear,
Just saying this:

Sweet dreams till sunbeams find you,
Sweet dreams that leave all worries behind you,
But in your dreams whatever they be,
Dream a little dream of me.

DREAMY

GETTING READY FOR BED DOESN'T JUST START the moment you say good night. These delicious dinners combine complex carbohydrates and protein and are very helpful in preparing the body for sleep *(see page 42)*. Scrambled Eggs and Cheese might be a classic breakfast, but did you know that it also contains valuable sleep agents, like eggs and milk? The more exotic Cold Sesame Noodles is a perfect late snack and hits with a triple tryptophan whammy of noodles, sesame seeds, and peanuts. You can't go wrong with the delicious and veggie-filled Tofu Stir-Fry, and by cutting back on the red meat, it'll be much easier to hit the hay. Enjoy these dishes or the simple suggestions in Quick Bites for a good night's sleep.

Scrambled Eggs and Cheese

2 eggs
1/4 cup milk
1/4 cup grated cheddar or Swiss cheese
salt and pepper to taste
1 tablespoon butter

1. Break the eggs into a bowl and add milk. Beat with a fork until frothy. Add cheese, salt, and pepper.
2. Have an adult heat the butter in a nonstick fry pan. When the butter has melted, turn the heat to low and pour in the egg mixture.
3. Move the eggs around with the back of the fork until they form soft curds. Serve eggs immediately.

Makes 2 servings.

Cold Sesame Noodles

1 (8-ounce) package of soba (lo mein) noodles or
    other thin pasta, cooked
6 tablespoons peanut butter or tahini sauce
1/4 cup hot water
2 tablespoons sesame oil
1/4 cup soy sauce
1/2 teaspoon ground ginger
1 clove garlic, minced
2–3 tablespoons green onions or chives, minced
1/2 cup bean sprouts

1. In a small bowl, whisk together the peanut butter or tahini sauce, hot water, sesame oil, soy sauce, ginger, and garlic until they form a creamy paste.
2. Toss the cooked noodles with the peanut butter paste in a large mixing bowl. Add green onions and bean sprouts.

DINNERS

3. Refrigerate and serve cold. Don't forget the chopsticks!

Makes 4 servings.

Tofu Stir-Fry

2 teaspoons each soy sauce, cornstarch,
    dry sherry, water
3 tablespoons peanut oil
1 garlic clove, minced
1 cup tofu cubes, drained
assorted vegetables cut into bite-size pieces
    (broccoli, asparagus, onion, etc.)
2 tablespoons water

Cooking sauce:
1/2 cup water or chicken broth
1 tablespoon dry sherry
2 tablespoons soy sauce or oyster sauce
1/4 teaspoon sugar
1 teaspoon sesame oil
1 tablespoon cornstarch

1. In a bowl, blend the soy sauce, cornstarch, sherry, water, and oil. Set aside.
2. In a separate bowl, mix the cooking sauce ingredients together. Set aside.
3. Have an adult heat a wok or large fry pan over high heat. Once the pan is hot, add 1 tablespoon oil. When oil begins to smoke, add garlic and stir.
4. Add vegetables and tofu and stir-fry for 30 seconds. Add 2 tablespoons water, cover, and cook for about 2 minutes for crisp vegetables, longer for tender vegetables.
5. Stir in cooking sauce and heat until sauce bubbles and thickens. Remove from the pan and serve immediately.

Makes 4 servings.

Quick Bites

Cooked pasta with a sprinkle of Parmesan cheese is an excellent light dinner.

Mix a handful of toasted sesame seeds with some salad greens. The greens don't help too much when it comes to promoting sleep, but they do contain calcium, and the sesame seeds contain tryptophan.

Fish with green vegetables also is great for dinner, since the magnesium and calcium are easily digested and relax the body.

The Dreamcatcher

Once upon a time, an old man sat upon a high mountaintop thinking about all of the things he had seen and done in his lifetime. Although he was satisfied with his life, he was afraid his children would not make the right decisions when he was gone.

Suddenly, he noticed a large, black spider crawling beside him. To his amazement, the spider began to speak to him.

"Do not be alarmed," said the spider, "I am not just a normal spider, but Iktomi." The old man was immediately filled with awe, since Iktomi was a wise, magical figure who had taught people many lessons.

"Iktomi," the old man began, "I am very old and content with life, but I'm afraid that when I leave this world, my children and people will be confused and unhappy."

Iktomi thought about this, then he scuttled around, collecting some rawhide, beads, feathers, and a switch from a willow tree. As he spoke, he bent the willow into a hoop and began weaving the rawhide to it.

"Life is like a big web," he said. "You begin your life as a little baby." Here he added a row of stitches around the outside of the hoop. "Then you become a child, then a young person, then an adult, and finally an old man, like you are now." He wove the rawhide into a web of circles that became smaller and smaller until there was just a hole in the middle. "It is all a big cycle that everyone must go through."

He tied the beads and feathers to the webbed hoop and gave it to the old man.

"But Iktomi, why is there a hole in the middle of your web?" asked the old man.

"A spider's web is beautiful to look at, but it is also very practical. The spider uses it to catch its dinner and nourish itself. In the course of your life, many things have affected the way you think and act. Some were good and some were bad. This web will catch all of the good dreams and visions of your people while they sleep. All of their nightmares and bad thoughts will fall through this hole and leave them forever. If they pay attention to the good things, they will be happy and their lives will be full of wisdom and joy."

The old man took the dreamcatcher and brought it back to his people. And from that time on, his people placed dreamcatchers above their beds and babies' cribs to remind themselves of life's harmony and cycle of renewal, and to catch all of their good dreams while letting their bad dreams float away.

CATCHING

You can catch fish and you can catch a cold, but did you know that you can also "catch" dreams? The legendary dreamcatcher, when hung above your bed, is said to capture your best dreams while you sleep. Make it with colorful lacing and add beads and feathers to create a beautiful decoration for your room that you can enjoy every night. And just like your dreams, each dreamcatcher is unique, with no two looking alike!

Dreamcatcher

Ruler, scissors, 4 yards suede lacing (from craft store), 5-inch diameter metal ring, glue, clothespin, 3 yards waxed nylon string about $1/8$-inch size, small beads of different colors, feathers

1. Measure and cut 8 inches of lacing. Glue one end of the lacing to the ring. Wrap the lacing around the ring until the entire ring is covered in a single layer, making sure not to twist the lacing. Glue the end and use the clothespin to hold it in place while it dries.

2. Tie one end of the waxed string to the ring. Make loose hitched knots all the way around the ring, with about a 1-inch space separating each knot. Make sure the string is tight where it loops around the ring. (see *figure a*)

3. When you get back to your first knot, keep making more hitch knots, looping them around the stitches you just made.

figure a

figure b

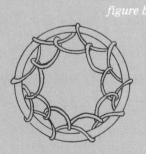

figure c

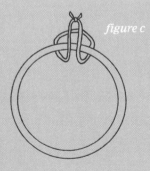

DREAMS

4. Continue until there is just a small hole in the center. Make a knot, add a drop of glue to it to make sure it doesn't untie, and then cut off any excess string. (see *figure b*)

5. Make the loop to hang your dreamcatcher by taking 12 inches of lacing, folding it in half, and knotting it close to the open end. Attach it to the top of the ring by slipping the loop through the ring, then around it and over the knot. Pull it tight. (see *figure c*)

6. Add beads to your dreamcatcher by cutting several pieces of lacing into 8-inch pieces. Tie the pieces to the sides of the ring, string beads on them, and then knot them tightly.

7. Add feathers by slipping them inside the beads and securing them with drops of glue.

Alice's Adventures in Wonderland

Lewis Carroll

Oh, I've had such a curious dream!" said Alice, and she told her sister, as well as she could remember them, all these strange Adventures of hers that you have just been reading about; and when she had finished, her sister kissed her, and said, "It *was* a curious dream, dear, certainly; but now run in to your tea; it's getting late." So Alice got up and ran off, thinking while she ran, as well she might, what a wonderful dream it had been.

Flying

I saw the moon,
One windy night,
Flying so fast—
All silvery white—
Over the sky
Like a toy balloon
Loose from its string—
A runaway moon.
The frosty stars
Went racing past,
Chasing her on
Ever so fast.
Then everyone said,
"It's the clouds that fly,
And the stars and the moon
Stand still in the sky."
But I don't mind—
I saw the moon
Sailing away
Like a toy
Balloon.

—*J.M. Westrup*

The Star Lovers

The king of the stars had one thoughtful and beautiful daughter. Her name was Orihime, her skin was as bright as a morning star, and her hair was as black as the night sky. Because she was his only daughter, she meant the world to the king, and he gave her the very important job of weaving the world's mist and clouds on an enormous loom. He would trust no one else to do it. She was a good daughter who always listened to the king and worked as hard as she could for him.

Orihime loved making the mist and clouds, but sometimes she would get tired of sitting at her loom all day long. "Father," she said one day, "I've made enough clouds and mist to last a month. May I please have one day to do whatever I want?" The king knew how hard she had worked, so he had no problem allowing her this one day off.

Orihime was very excited to finally have a day to relax. She decided to spend it wading in the Milky Way, the stream of stars that ran through the sky, and playing on its shores. She splashed in the stars and was so busy having fun that she didn't notice the young man who was admiring her on the other side of the stream.

She suddenly became self-conscious and turned to go. The young man called out, "I'm sorry to stare at you. I've never seen anyone look as happy as you look right now. My name is Kengyu and I am the servant who watches the king's star cattle." He shyly looked down. "Would it be all right if I stayed here awhile?"

Kengyu looked so friendly that Orihime agreed, and they spent the whole day walking along the Milky Way, talking, keeping an eye on the star cattle, and having a good time. In fact, they were having such a good time that Orihime didn't notice how late it had gotten. She hurried back home as fast as she could and just made it in time for dinner.

The next day, she began working on the mist and clouds again, but all the time she was thinking of Kengyu. "I wonder if he's thinking about me," she mused. She was so distracted with imagining what Kengyu was doing that she ended up weaving mist that was green and clouds that trailed long threads from their ends. Her father was not happy with her work.

"This is how you repay me for letting you go yesterday?" He scolded her.

Orihime thought of a plan. "Father, I don't feel very well. I think I might have caught a cold wading in the Milky Way." Although the king of the stars was a strict parent, he loved his daughter very much and didn't want her to get sick.

So, he agreed to let her go home and rest for another day.

After she left her father, Orihime quickly walked to the Milky Way. Sure enough, there was Kengyu tending the cattle. When he saw her, his whole face lit up. "Orihime, I thought I would never see you again!" he exclaimed as he waded through the stars. "So did I," said Orihime. They spent the whole day together and had even more fun than the time before. Orihime wanted to stay with Kengyu forever.

Unfortunately, Orihime forgot all about her loom and her father. The king was surprised to find that there were no more clouds to make the rain and mists to blanket the ground, but what surprised him even more was the sight of the abandoned loom.

"Where has Orihime gone?" he puzzled. Then he heard her sweet laughter coming from the Milky Way. Fast as lightning, he flew to where the lovers were sitting and scolded Orihime. "Because you lied to me, you will never see Kengyu again," he declared. Then he turned the little stream of stars that was the Milky Way into a huge, roaring torrent. There was no way the lovers could wade across the steam now to see each other.

Even though his daughter pleaded and begged to return, the king of the stars thought that once he had separated them, Orihime would concentrate on her work. But all she did was sit at the loom and cry, thinking about all the fun she was missing being apart from Kengyu. Kengyu wasn't doing much better. All of the star cattle wandered off because he wasn't paying attention to them. He was too distracted by thoughts of Orihime.

Now, on top of having no new clouds or mist woven, the king of the stars had a crying daughter and a depressed servant, and all of his star cattle were lost! He knew that he would have to resolve this issue somehow, so he thought and thought. Finally, he went to Orihime and took her hands in his. "Orihime, I realize how much you care for Kengyu and it was wrong of me to separate you two. But you have to realize that the earth needs clouds and mist to provide rain and moisture. You must continue weaving!"

Orihime wiped away her tears and carefully thought about this. Finally she said, "I will weave your mist and clouds, but you must let me see Kengyu at least once a month."

Realizing this was the only way to make everyone happy, the king grudgingly accepted. Orihime was so overjoyed that she kissed him and set to work at her loom, making more clouds and mist then she had ever done before. When the time came to visit Kengyu, her father was true to his word and arranged for a boat to take her across. And so, once a month the star lovers are reunited.

St. Judy's Comet

By Paul Simon

Oo, little sleepy boy,
Do you know what time it is?
Well, the hour of your bedtime's long been past,
And though I know you're fightin' it,
I can tell when you rub your eyes,
You're fadin' fast, oh, fadin' fast.

Won't you run come see St. Judy's Comet
Roll across the skies,
And leave a spray of diamonds in its wake.
I long to see St. Judy's Comet
Sparkle in your eyes when you awake,
Oh, when you wake, wake.

Little boy, little boy,
Won't you lay your body down.
Little boy, little boy,
Won't you close your weary eyes.
Ain't nothin' flashin' but the fireflies.

Well, I sang it once, and I sang it twice,
I'm goin' to sing it three times more,
I'm goin' to stay 'til your resistance
Is overcome,
'Cause if I can't sing my boy to sleep,
Well, it makes your famous daddy look so dumb,
look so dumb.

Won't you run come see St. Judy's Comet
Roll across the skies,
And leave a spray of diamonds in its wake.

I long to see St. Judy's Comet
Sparkle in your eyes when you awake,
Oh, when you wake, wake.

Little boy, little boy,
Won't you lay your body down.
Little boy, little boy
Won't you close your weary eyes.
Ain't nothin' flashin' but the fireflies.

Oo, little sleepy boy
Do you know what time it is?
Well, the hour of your bedtime's long been past,
And though I know you're fightin' it,
I can tell when you rub your eyes
That you're fadin' fast, oo, fadin' fast.

The Sugar-Plum Tree

Have you ever heard of the Sugar-Plum tree?
'Tis a tree of great renown:
It blooms on the shore of the Lollipop sea,
In the garden of Shut-Eye town.
The fruit that it bears is so wondrously sweet,
(As those who have tasted it say)
That good little children have only to eat
Of that fruit, to be happy next day.

There are marshmallows, gum-drops,
and peppermint canes,
With stripings of scarlet and gold,
And you carry away of the treasure that rains
As much as your apron will hold:
So come, little child, cuddle closer to me
In your dainty white night-cap and gown,
And I'll rock you away to that Sugar-Plum tree,
In the garden of Shut-Eye town.

—*Eugene Field*

Sweet

THESE FANTASTIC COOKIES ARE SO GOOD, they are absolutely dreamy. Basic Almond Cookies are turned into full-moon cookies that you can transform into half-moons and crescents, and then make disappear. Lemon Star Cookies are pretty to look at and are so light and sweet while you eat, they practically melt on your tongue. Oatmeal-and-Raisin Cookies are classic, but did you know that the complex carbohydrates they contain could help you get to sleep faster? You might not be able to eat Overnight Surprise Cookies before bedtime, but they'll be magically baking away while you sleep through the night. And finally, a cup of cocoa is a sweet and cozy treat, but add a few marshmallow stars and it becomes cosmically delicious!

Full-Moon Cookies
1 cup almonds, sliced
1 1/2 sticks butter, softened
1/4 cup sugar
1 large egg
2 teaspoons almond extract
1 1/4 cups all-purpose flour
1/2 teaspoon ground nutmeg

1. Make sure the oven rack is in the center of the oven. Preheat to 350°F.
2. Blend the sugar and butter together in a bowl. Stop when it's light and fluffy.
3. Add the egg to the mixture and mix until it is well blended. Add the almond extract and mix again.
4. Add half the flour and mix until smooth. Add the rest of the flour and the nutmeg and mix.
5. Add and mix the almond slices, crumbling

them into smaller pieces before distributing them. The mixture should be doughy now.
6. Take a piece of dough about the size of your palm and make a ball. Then flatten it into a "full moon." Place moons on a cookie sheet at least 1 1/2 inches apart (they'll expand in the oven).
7. Using oven mitts, carefully slide cookie sheet onto the middle oven rack. Bake for 10–12 minutes, or until the edges are golden.
8. Carefully remove the sheet with mitts, and place cookies on cooling rack. Wait for cookies to cool, and then enjoy.

Makes a dozen cookies.

Lemon Star Cookies
1 cup butter, softened
3/4 cup sugar
1 egg
1 teaspoon vanilla extract
2 3/4 cups all-purpose flour

Treats

1 teaspoon baking soda
1 teaspoon cream of tartar
2 teaspoons grated lemon peel
orange and yellow food
   coloring
2 star-shaped cookie cutters, one large, one small

1. Preheat oven to 350°F.
2. Mix the butter and sugar in a large bowl until light and fluffy. Add the egg and beat well, then add the vanilla extract.
3. Mix the flour, baking soda, cream of tartar, and lemon peel together in another bowl. Combine the contents of the two bowls, mixing carefully a little at a time to blend well.
4. Divide the dough into two lumps. Add a few drops of yellow food coloring to one lump and knead it well. Repeat with orange food coloring for the other lump of dough. If the dough doesn't seem firm enough afterward, try refrigerating it for a few hours to make it firm enough to cut.
5. Sprinkle some flour on a piece of wax paper laid out on a counter or table. Using a rolling pin, flatten out the yellow dough on top. Use the large cookie cutter to cut out as many big star shapes as you can. Discard excess dough.

6. Use the small cookie cutter to cut out a small star from the center of each large yellow star. You should now have a bunch of small yellow stars and a bunch of large yellow stars with star-shaped holes in their centers. Put these large and small yellow stars to the side.
7. Flatten and cut out the orange dough exactly as with the yellow. You should now have two batches of big stars (orange and yellow) with star-shaped holes, and two batches of small stars (orange and yellow).

8. To assemble the cookies, place a large orange star on a baking sheet. Place a small yellow star in the star-shaped hole at the center. Pinch the edges of the big orange star and the small yellow star together to make sure they don't separate when baking.

9. Repeat for each big and little star piece.

10. Once you've created all of your stars, use oven mitts to slide the cookie sheet into the oven. Bake for 10–12 minutes. Remove cookies and place on cooling rack.

Makes 3 dozen cookies.

Overnight Surprise Cookies

2 egg whites
3/4 cup sugar
1 cup pecans, sliced
1 cup chocolate chips

1. Preheat oven to 350°F.

2. Mix together egg whites and sugar a small amount at a time, until thoroughly blended and stiffly peaked.

3. Mix in pecans and chocolate chips.

4. Place pieces of dough, each about an inch wide, on a baking sheet. Leave at least a space of 1 1/2 inch between each cookie.

5. Use oven mitts to slide the cookie sheet onto the oven rack. Then shut the door and

turn off the oven. Repeat: Make sure that you turn the oven off!

6. Don't open the oven door until the next morning when you wake up. A delicious surprise will be waiting for you!

Makes a dozen cookies.

Oatmeal-and-Raisin Cookies

2 sticks butter, softened
1 cup brown sugar, packed
1/2 cup sugar
2 eggs
1 teaspoon vanilla extract
1 1/2 cups all-purpose flour
1 teaspoon baking soda
1 teaspoon ground cinnamon
1/2 teaspoon salt
3 cups quick-cooking rolled oats
1 cup raisins

1. Preheat oven to 350°F.

2. In a large bowl, blend butter and sugars until light and fluffy.

3. Add eggs and vanilla. Beat well.

4. Using a separate bowl, combine flour, baking soda, cinnamon, and salt. Add butter a little at a time to the mixture and blend well.

5. Add oats and raisins. Mix well.

6. Using a tablespoon, drop dough onto a

greased cookie sheet, one at a time, about 2 inches apart.

7. Use the mitts to slide the tray into the oven and bake for 10–12 minutes, or until lightly browned.

8. Remove tray and transfer cookies to a cooling rack.

Makes 4 dozen cookies.

Starry Marshmallow Cocoa

milk (whole or skim) or water
instant cocoa
marshmallows
very small star-shaped cookie cutter

1. Follow the instructions on the instant cocoa packet, and mix together milk or water and cocoa. Heat on low in a medium saucepan until well blended and hot.

2. Using a rolling pin, carefully flatten a marshmallow and then cut out a star shape using the cookie cutter. Repeat for as many star marshmallows as you want.

3. Add the marshmallows to the hot chocolate, and enjoy.

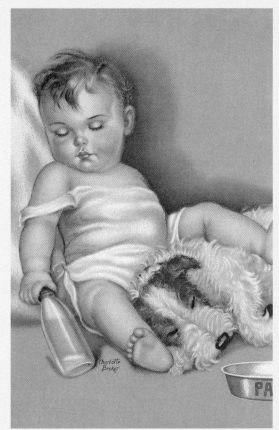

Sleepy Tots

Sleepy Tots
Come close each eye
And sing a little lullabye

Softly nods
Each downy head
On its drowsy way to bed

Nodding
In the candle light
When it's time to say good night.

Our little party of travellers awakened the next morning refreshed and full of hope, and Dorothy breakfasted like a princess off peaches and plums from the trees beside the river. Behind them was the dark forest they had passed safely through, although they had suffered many discouragements; but before them was a lovely, sunny country that seemed to beckon them on to the Emerald City.

To be sure, the broad river now cut them off from this beautiful land; but the raft was nearly done, and after the Tin Woodman had cut a few more logs and fastened them together with wooden pins, they were ready to start. Dorothy sat down in the middle of the raft and held Toto in her arms. When the Cowardly Lion stepped upon the raft it tipped badly, for he was big and heavy; but the Scarecrow and the Tin Woodman stood upon the other end to steady it, and they had long poles in their hands to push the raft through the water.

They got along quite well at first, but when they reached the middle of the river the swift current swept the raft downstream, farther and farther away from the road of yellow brick; and the water grew so deep that the long poles would not touch the bottom.

"This is bad," said the Tin Woodman, "for if we cannot get to the land we shall be carried into the country of the Wicked Witch of the West, and she will enchant us and make us her slaves."

"And then I should get no brains," said the Scarecrow.

"And I should get no courage," said the Cowardly Lion.

"And I should get no heart," said the Tin Woodman.

"And I should never get back to Kansas," said Dorothy.

"We must certainly get to the Emerald City if we can," the Scarecrow continued, and he pushed so hard on his long pole that it stuck fast in the mud at the bottom of the river, and before he could pull it out again, or let go, the raft was swept away and the poor Scarecrow left clinging to the pole in the middle of the river. . . . Down the stream the raft floated, and the poor Scarecrow was left far behind. Then the Lion said:

"Something must be done to save us. I think I can swim to the shore and pull the raft after me, if you will only hold fast to the tip of my tail."

So he sprang into the water and the Tin Woodman caught fast hold of his tail, when the Lion began to swim with all his might toward the shore. It was hard work, although he was so big; but by and by they were drawn out of the current, and then Dorothy took the Tin Woodman's long pole and helped push the raft to the land.

They were all tired out when they reached the shore at last and stepped off upon the pretty green grass, and they also knew that the stream had carried them a long way past the road of yellow brick that led to the Emerald City.

"What shall we do now?" asked the Tin Woodman, as the Lion lay down on the grass to let the sun dry him.

"We must get back to the road, in some way," said Dorothy.

"The best plan will be to walk along the riverbank until we come to the road again," remarked the Lion. . . . They walk along as fast as they could, Dorothy only stopping once to pick a beautiful flower; and after a time the Tin Woodman cried out: "Look!"

Then they all looked at the river and saw the Scarecrow perched upon his pole in the middle of the water, looking very lonely and sad.

"What can we do to save him?" asked Dorothy.

The Lion and the Woodman both shook their heads, for they did not know. So they sat down upon the bank and gazed wistfully at the Scarecrow until a Stork flew by, which, seeing them, stopped to rest at the water's edge.

"Who are you and where are you going?" asked the Stork.

"I am Dorothy," answered the girl, "and these are my friends, the Tin Woodman and the Cowardly Lion; and we are going to the Emerald City."

"This isn't the road," said the Stork, as she twisted her long neck and looked sharply at the queer party.

"I know it," returned Dorothy, "But we have lost the Scarecrow, and are wondering how we shall get him again."

"Where is he?" asked the Stork.

"Over there in the river," answered the girl.

"If he wasn't so big and heavy I would get him for you," remarked the Stork.

"He isn't heavy a bit," said Dorothy eagerly, "for he is stuffed with straw; and if you will bring him back to us we shall thank you ever and ever so much."

"Well, I'll try," said the Stork, "but if I find he is too heavy to carry I shall have to drop him in the river again."

So the big bird flew into the air and over the water till she came to where the Scarecrow was perched upon his pole. Then the Stork with her great claws grabbed the Scarecrow by the arm and carried him up into the air and back to the bank, where Dorothy and the Lion and the Tin Woodman and Toto were sitting.

When the Scarecrow found himself among his friends again he was so happy that he hugged them all, even the Lion and Toto; and as they walked along he sang "Tol-de-ri-de-oh!" at every step, he felt so gay.

"I was afraid I should have to stay in the river forever," he said, "but the kind Stork saved me, and if I ever get any brains I shall find the Stork again and do it some kindness in return."

"That's all right," said the Stork, who was flying along beside them. "I always like to help anyone in trouble. But I must go now, for my babies are waiting in the nest for me. I hope you will find the Emerald City and that Oz will help you."

"Thank you," replied Dorothy, and then the kind Stork flew into the air and was soon out of sight.

They walked along listening to the singing of the bright-coloured birds and looking at the lovely flowers which now became so thick that the ground was carpeted with them. There were big yellow and white and blue and purple blossoms, besides great clusters of scarlet poppies, which were so brilliant in colour they almost dazzled Dorothy's eyes.

"Aren't they beautiful?" the girl asked, as she breathed in the spicy scent of the flowers.

"I suppose so," answered the Scarecrow. "When I have brains I shall probably like them better."

"If I only had a heart I should love them," added the Tin Woodman.

"I always did like flowers, "said the Lion; "they seem so helpless and frail. But there are none in the forest so bright as these."

They now came upon more and more of the big scarlet poppies, and fewer and fewer of the other flowers; and soon they found themselves in the midst of a great meadow of poppies. Now it is well known that when there are many of these flowers together their odour is so powerful that anyone who breathes it falls asleep, and if the sleeper is not carried away from the scent of the flowers he sleeps on and on forever. But Dorothy did not know this, nor could she get away from the bright red flowers that were everywhere about; so presently her eyes grew heavy and she felt she must sit down to rest and to sleep.

But the Tin Woodman would not let her do this.

"We must hurry and get back to the road of yellow brick before dark," he said; and the Scarecrow agreed with him. So they kept walking until Dorothy could stand no longer. Her eyes closed in spite of herself and she forgot where she was and fell among the poppies, fast asleep.

"What shall we do?" asked the Tin Woodman.

"If we leave her here she will die," said the Lion. "The smell of the flowers is killing us all. I myself can scarcely keep my eyes open and the dog is asleep already."

It was true; Toto had fallen down beside his little mistress. But the Scarecrow and the Tin Woodman, not being made out of flesh, were not troubled by the scent of the flowers.

"Run fast," said the Scarecrow to the Lion, "and get out of this deadly flower bed as soon as you can. We will bring the little girl with us, but if you should fall asleep you are too big to be carried."

So the Lion aroused himself and bounded forward as fast as he could go. In a moment he was out of sight.

"Let us make a chair with our hands, and carry her," said the Scarecrow. So they picked up Toto and put the dog in Dorothy's lap, and then they made a chair with their hands for the seat and their arms for the arms and carried the sleeping girl between them through the flowers. . . . They carried the sleeping girl to a pretty spot beside the river, far enough from the poppy field to prevent her breathing any more of the poison of the flowers, and her they laid her gently on the soft grass and waited for the fresh breeze to waken her. ☾

SLEEPY

Some sounds, like the gentle roar of waves, are very relaxing. And some foods, like milk or turkey, can make you feel sleepy. But did you know that there are actually some smells that might help you go to sleep at night? It's true. Ever since ancient times, different cultures have used natural scents to do a number of things, from soothing minds to providing energy. Using oils and scents that come from natural plants to help your mind and body is called aromatherapy. Lavender and sandalwood are just two of the essential oils that have a calming and relaxing effect on your mind. And when your mind is calm, it's much easier to drift off to sleep. Try out one of these aromatic ideas the next time you have trouble sleeping.

Sleep-Inducing Ingredients

Bergamot, clary sage, chamomile, geranium, jasmine, lavender, marjoram, neroli, roman chamomile, rose, sandalwood

Use any one or a combination of these herbs or flowers in your potpourri. Many of these scents are also available as essential oils.

Because essential oils are very concentrated, don't put them directly on your skin (they're not perfumes). Try adding about four drops of essential oil to your nighttime bath or using handmade scented soaps. You can also sprinkle a few drops of oil on a tissue or handkerchief, then tuck it into your pillowcase. The sweet scent of chamomile tea before bedtime is also very relaxing.

A Good-Night Sachet

Large linen or cotton handkerchief, potpourri (see Sleep-Inducing Ingredients), rubber band, ribbon with a width of 1/4 inch or less

1. Place a handful of potpourri in the middle of handkerchief.
2. Gather the sides together above the potpourri and secure with the rubber band.
3. Place ribbon over the rubber band and tie into a pretty bow.
4. Place the sachet on or near your bed for sweet dreams. Or use a longer ribbon to hang sachet from the bed frame.

SCENTS

5. Refill sachet when smell diminishes or when you want a new scent.

Sleepytime Suds

Six bars of pure glycerin soap, cutting board, knife, heavy pot, lavender essential oil, glass pie plate or candy molds, ladle, lavender sprigs or rose petals

1. Cut soap into small chunks and melt in the pot over medium heat for 15 minutes. Don't stir.
2. Add three drops of the lavender essential oil to the bottom of the pie plate or candy molds.
3. Once the soap has melted, carefully ladle it into the pie plate or molds. Don't let the soap bubble or foam. If it does, turn off the heat.
4. When the soap cools, it will set and harden. Wait until it begins to cool, then press a few sprigs of lavender or rose petals onto the surface.
5. Melt some more soap. Pour it on top of the cooled layer to seal the herbs or petals in the middle of the soap.
6. When the soap has hardened, cut into bars or remove from molds.

ROCK-A-BYE, BABY

Rock-a-bye, baby,
On the treetop,
When the wind blows,
The cradle will rock;
When the bough breaks,
The cradle will fall,
And down will come baby,
Cradle and all.

Sweet & Low

Sweet and low, sweet and low,
Wind of the western sea,
Low, low, breathe and blow,
Wind of the western sea!
Over the rolling waters go,
Come from the dying moon, and blow,
Blow him again to me
While my little one, while my pretty one
Sleeps.

Sleep and rest, sleep and rest,
Father will come to thee soon;
Rest, rest, on mother's breast,
Father will come to thee soon;
Father will come to his babe in the nest,
Silver sails all out of the west
Under the silver moon.
Sleep, my little one, sleep, my pretty one,
Sleep.

—*Alfred, Lord Tennyson*

RELAXATION

Sometimes it's difficult to go to sleep. You toss and turn, you try to find a comfy place in your bed, but it just doesn't work. Maybe you're nervous about something, or maybe you feel like you have too many thoughts running through your head. Meditation is something that everyone can do and can help get your mind relaxed and ready for sleep. Try one or two of these exercises together to help you calm down and relax before bedtime. Don't be discouraged if they don't work immediately. Sometimes it takes a little practice. And you might want to use them during the day whenever you feel tense, too!

Muscle Relaxation

1. Lie down with your arms at your sides and take a few deep breaths.
2. Point your fingers as you stretch your arms. Hold them like that for two deep breaths.
3. Slowly relax your arms.
4. Point your toes and stretch your legs. Hold for two breaths, then slowly relax.
5. Repeat this again for your arms and legs, taking the time to slowly relax.

6. Bend your knees into your chest and curl into a ball. Wrap your arms around your knees and tuck your head into your legs.
7. Tighten all of your muscles and hold them as you breathe in. When you breathe out, slowly let your body relax and uncurl.
8. Curl into a ball once more, and repeat the exercise.
9. Take a few deep, even breaths, and let your whole body go limp.

Visualization

1. Close your eyes.
2. Imagine yourself in a special place. It could be the beach or the woods or your grandmother's house. It could be a real place or a place you made up. Just make sure it's anywhere you feel safe and comfortable.
3. Pretend that you are actually in that place. If you are at the beach, try to feel the soft sand beneath your feet. Hear the wind rustling the leaves of the trees. Try to make it as real as possible.
4. Breathe slowly and evenly. Feel what it is

EXERCISES

like to be in this special place, completely safe and content.

5. When you want to return to your bedroom, slowly count backward from 5. When you reach 1, slowly open your eyes and take a breath. Wiggle your toes and fingers.

6. Remember that you can visit this special place any time you want.

Deep Breathing

1. Lie on your back and put one hand on your stomach over your belly button. Put your other hand on top of this hand.

2. Slowly take a deep breath. Imagine your lungs and diaphragm, the muscle under your lungs, filling up with air. Your hands should rise slightly.

3. Now slowly release your breath. Your hands should fall slightly as the air leaves your lungs and diaphragm.

4. Keep working on breathing slowly and deeply, and making your hands on your stomach move up and down. Don't try to force your breathing.

5. Try to breathe like this 10 times in a row. Stop immediately if you start to get dizzy—this means you are breathing too deeply or too quickly.

The Princess & the Pea

Once upon a time there was a handsome Prince who lived in a big stone castle with his father and mother, the King and Queen. He had everything a young man could want: wealth, good looks, and all the sweets he could eat! And yet, the Prince was very sad. He wandered around the castle halls day and night, leaving behind him a fresh trail of tear drops.

The King and Queen were very worried about their son. One evening, they begged him to explain what was wrong.

"You have everything a young man could want. What could be causing you such despair?" pleaded his mother.

"I have everything but the one thing I most long for: True love. I wish to have a princess at my side and a family of my own," said the Prince.

The King and Queen agreed it was finally time for their son to marry. But there were no princesses left in all the kingdom for their dear Prince to woo. So they decided to send him on a journey around the world, where he might find the princess of his dreams.

The Prince was gone for many days and many nights. He visited far away cities and towns, from China to Peru, and met many nice princesses. Some were beautiful, some were kind, some were funny, and others quite serious. But none of them captured the Prince's heart. You see, there is no formula for why two people fall in love; it's one of the greatest mysteries. But the Prince felt sure he'd know when he found the right young lady.

All gloom and doom, the Prince returned home to his mother and father, who consoled him with a hundred hugs and kisses.

Some days later, a terrible storm raged across the land, shaking the walls with booming CRACKS of thunder, and charging the sky with enormous BOLTS of lightning. As the Prince lay in his bed that night, staring hopelessly out the window, he heard a banging on the castle's front door. Wrapping himself in a blanket, he descended the long winding staircase to the entry hall. BANG! BANG! BANG! The knocking grew louder and louder. As he pulled open the heavy wooden door it let out a loud CREAK. Standing there before him was a young woman soaked from head to toe and shivering from the freezing rain. As the Prince raised his eyes to meet the girl's gaze, he fell instantly head over heels in love.

"Come in, dear lady, come in," said the Prince and ushered her into the front parlor, where he wrapped her in his blanket and fed her hot chocolate with extra whipped cream. The King and Queen awoke and rushed down to see what all the commotion was about.

Through chattering teeth, the young woman introduced herself as Princess Angeline. She had been traveling home from a trip with her chaperone when he was struck down by lightening and killed. Lost and alone, she wandered along the road, till she found herself at the walls of the castle. She thanked the King and Queen for their hospitality and, especially, the Prince, whom she couldn't take her eyes off of.

The Queen could see her son was smitten with this beautiful girl, but how could she be certain the girl was telling the truth about being a princess? Suddenly, she thought of a way to test the girl's honesty. She called in one of her maids and instructed her to place a single pea under a pile of ten mattresses in the guest room, where Angeline was to sleep. Then the Queen showed the young lady to her bed, and bid a her a good night's rest.

Angeline had never seen such a tall bed! But she didn't wish to offend her hosts, so she climbed to the very top and tucked herself in.

That night the Prince dreamt only of the beautiful Princess. But the Princess did not dream of anything at all. In fact, she barely slept a wink the whole night long!

The next morning, as the Princess joined the royal family for breakfast, the Queen asked her politely, "My dear, did you have a pleasant rest?"

"Madame, I do not wish to sound ungrateful, but that was the most uncomfortable bed I've ever slept in! I felt as though I were lying upon a huge jagged rock, and awoke all sore and covered with bruises."

"Ah-hah!" the Queen exclaimed, as she clapped her hands together, for she knew that this girl must be a princess if she had the sensitivity to feel the pea beneath all those mattresses.

Two weeks later, the Prince asked the Princess to marry him, and she accepted. On their wedding day, the Prince presented the Princess with a special gift, a beautiful gold necklace with an unusual sparkling ball dangling from the end of the chain. You see, it was that very same pea she'd slept on, dipped in real gold, and covered with glittering diamonds!

From that day forward, the Princess never took that necklace off. And she and her Prince lived happily ever after.

from The Bed Book

Most Beds are Beds
For sleeping or resting,
But the *best* Beds are much
   More interesting!

Not just a white little
Tucked-in-tight little
Nighty-nighty little
Turn-out-the-light little
   Bed—

Instead
A Bed for Fishing,
A Bed for Cats,
A Bed for a Troupe of
   Acrobats.

The *right* sort of Bed
(If you see what I mean)
Is a Bed that might
   Be a Submarine

Nosing through water
Clear and green,
Silver and glittery
   As a sardine.

Or a Jet-Propelled Bed
For visiting Mars
With mosquito nets
For the shooting stars...

—*Sylvia Plath*

DREAM

Surround yourself with wonderful dreams every single night with this cozy quilt you can create with a special adult. Making the quilt will take some time, so don't worry about finishing it all at one sitting. Try making a new square every week, or maybe one a night as part of a bedtime ritual. Once you're done with the squares, ask an adult to sew them all together. Your patience will pay off when you find yourself with a gorgeous quilt made up of all your favorite dreams!

For Fabric Squares:
Fabric pieces cut into 4¹/₂" x 4¹/₂" squares; fabric markers, fabric crayons, or fabric paint; additional pieces of fabric; scissors; large needle; embroidery thread

Decorate your squares with fabric markers, crayons, or paint, or cut and sew on fabric shapes. You can even sew pictures on the squares with a large needle and embroidery thread. Use themes related to sleep or nighttime, like beds, sheep, stars, moons, comets, planets, or outer-space objects. Finally, decorate other squares with pictures of happy

dreams, or wishes and dreams you have for the future.

For Quilt:
Scissors, iron, straight pins, needle, thread, 66" x 96" twin flat sheet, thin quilt batting or flannel fabric, darning needle, wool yarn

1. Iron squares and arrange them on the floor in 24 rows of 18 squares each, creating a pleasing pattern.
2. To sew the first row, place the second square on top of the first, front sides facing each other. Pin along one side of the square and sew a ¼-inch seam down this side. Remove pins.
3. Unfold the first and second squares along the seam and lay them right side up. Pin and sew the third square to the second square, again with the front sides together, so that you are making a row with the seams on the bottom when unfolded. Continue until all 18 squares are sewn, then do another row
4. With front sides facing each other, pin and sew the first and second rows together along

QUILT

one edge. Repeat until all 24 rows are sewn together. This is your quilt top. Turn the top upside down and iron all seams open.

5. Place your batting or flannel material on the backside of the quilt top and stitch it loosely to hold it together (these stitches may be removed later.)

6. Smooth the bedsheet out on the floor and center your quilt on top of the sheet, front side down, batting facing up. Pin together.

7. Sew a ¼-inch seam around your quilt, leaving a 6-inch opening in the middle of one side. Remove pins.

8. Turn your quilt right side out through the opening. Stitch opening closed.

9. Iron the quilt and lay it out on the floor. Hold the thickness of the quilt together using pins. Push the darning needle threaded with wool yarn through the middle of a quilt square, leaving about 5 inches of yarn on top. Push the needle back through the quilt from back to front and cut the yarn, leaving another 5 inches. Tie the pieces of yarn together in a square knot. Trim ends. Repeat in the middle of each square. Remove pins.

A Midsummer

Oberon went, unperceived by Titania, to her bower, where she was preparing to go to rest. Her fairy bower was a bank, where grew wild thyme, cowslips, and sweet violets under a canopy of woodbine, musk-roses, and eglantine. There Titania always slept some part of the night; her coverlet the enameled skin of a snake, which, though a small mantle, was wide enough to wrap a fairy in.

He found Titania giving orders to her fairies, how they were to employ themselves while she slept. "Some of you," said her majesty, "must kill cankers in the musk-rose-buds, and some wage war with the bats for their leathern wings, to make my small elves coats; and some of you keep watch that the clamorous owl, that nightly hoots, comes not near me; but first sing me to sleep." Then they began to sing this song:

Night's Dream

William Shakespeare, retold by Charles and Mary Lamb

"You spotted snakes with double tongue,
Thorny hedgehogs, be not seen;
Newts and blind-worms, do no wrong,
Come out near our Fairy Queen.
Philomel, with melody,
Sing in your sweet lullaby,
Lulla, lulla, lullaby; lulla, lulla, lullaby:
Never harm, nor spell, nor charm,
Come our lovely lady nigh;
So good-night with lullaby."

When the fairies had sung their queen with this pretty lullaby, they left her, to perform the important services she had enjoined them. Oberon then softly drew near his Titania, and dropped some of the love-juice on her eyelids, saying,
"What thou seest, when thou dost wake,
Do it for thy true-love sake."

Angels bless and angels keep
Angels guard me while I sleep
Bless my heart and bless my home
Bless my spirit as I roam
Guide and guard me through the night
and wake me with the morning's light.

—*Traditional*

May all the beings in all the worlds be happy.
May all the beings in all the worlds be happy.
May all the beings in all the worlds be happy.
Om Peace, Peace, Peace.

—*from the Vedas*

Anansi Finds the Moon

A long, long time ago, Anansi the spider lived with his six children in a little house. Anansi wasn't just any ordinary spider, but a very tricky character who cleverly got himself into (and out of) many adventures. One morning, Anansi woke up and realized it was such a beautiful day, he would like to visit the town.

"I'll only be gone a few hours," he told his children. "Make sure you stay close to the house."

He gathered his things and was off.

A few hours went by and the children began to worry about their father. The day wore on, and they thought that maybe something bad had happened to him.

"Perhaps a tiger ate him!" said one.

"A tiger? He'd barely be a mouthful for a tiger," said another, "He probably met a snake that gobbled him up!"

"Maybe someone squashed him!" cried another.

While they argued about what might have happened to their father, one little spider who had very good eyesight climbed a tall tree and looked into the distance. He yelled to his brothers and sister, "I see father! He has fallen into the river! Quick, we must help him!"

Immediately, the biggest spider pulled his brothers and sister onto his back and swung on the end of a spider thread to the river. There he let them off, and the clever sister spider made a life preserver out of a nut and threw it to her father. Anansi clung to it while the spider—child who was the best swimmer hauled him toward shore.

But just as they reached the riverbank, a big bird swooped down and carried Anansi off! Truth be told, the bird thought she was just picking up a nut and didn't know Anansi was holding on for dear life. Thinking quickly, the youngest spider picked up a smooth rock and threw it at the bird. The bird squawked and dropped the nut, and luckily, the chubbiest spider—child was there to cushion Anansi's fall.

Everyone started walking toward home, cheering and feeling very good about themselves. *What wonderful children I have!* thought Anansi as he wondered how he could reward them.

As they were walking back, Anansi almost tripped over a strange object half—buried in the dirt. When he dug it out, he saw that it was a beautiful, silvery orb. He and his children had no idea where it came from, but they admired the shining object. Right there and then, Anansi promised to give the glowing ball to the child who most deserved it after dinner that evening. He placed the ball in his garden until then.

The rest of the day was nothing but fighting! Each of the children wanted the glowing ball, so each of them was completely certain that they had played the key part in rescuing their father.

"If not for me, we wouldn't even have known what happened to him!" said the spider who had first spied Anansi in the river.

The biggest spider snorted. "But we would have gotten there too late if I hadn't been strong enough to carry you all to the river!"

"Please!" said the sister spider. "Dad would have been swept away if I hadn't turned that nut into a life preserver and thrown it to him. I'm a genius!"

The swimmer spider yelled, "Yeah right! Just forget about how I jumped in and courageously pulled Dad to safety! I still have water in my ear!"

The youngest spider sniffled. "I was the one who threw the rock that startled the bird into dropping Dad!"

"But I was the one who caught. . .er, cushioned him," said the chubbiest brother.

The children argued so much that Anansi covered his ears and shook his head. The beautiful globe was lovely, but was it worth all of this fighting? He was so busy arguing with his children that he didn't notice the big bird gently land in his garden. The bird was very angry about having that stone thrown at her, and so she had followed the spider family home, waiting to play a trick on them to get them back. When she saw the beautiful globe in the garden, she knew exactly what she'd do. Quietly, she lifted the globe up and flew high, high, high in the air. She placed it among the stars, knowing Anansi and his little family would never be able to reach it.

Anansi came out to get the silvery ball, but couldn't find it anywhere. He looked all over, but it seemed to have just disappeared. Then he noticed it hanging way, way up in the sky.

"Hey Dad," said one of his children as they came outside, "what happened to that great ball?" Another one noticed it in the sky, "How'd it get up there?"

"Oh, um," Anansi tried to think fast. "I put it up there! All of you were bickering so much that I decided to put it in the sky so you could all look at it and share it equally."

His children realized that they been fighting for no good reason and apologized to one another. They all thought what Anansi had done was very clever, and they all agreed the ball made a wonderful light in the starry sky. The little family stood in the moonlight admiring its glow, not realizing how the moon had really gotten up there. To this day, the only ones who really know are the angry bird and Anansi the spider, and HE'S certainly not telling!

who knows if the moon's

who knows if the moon's
a balloon, coming out of a keen city
in the sky — filled with pretty people?
(and if you and i should

get into it, if they
should take me and take you into their balloon,
why then
we'd go up higher with all the pretty people

than houses and steeples and clouds:
go sailing
away and away sailing into a keen
city which nobody's ever visited, where

always
    it's
        Spring) and everyone's
in love and flowers pick themselves

—e.e. cummings

The Legend of Heng O

Once upon a time, in the heavenly court of the Jade Emperor, a beautiful servant named Heng O broke a very valuable vase and was sent to earth as punishment. There she lived with a poor family until the day she met Hou Yi, the most famous archer in the land. He fell in love with her immediately, and they got married.

Now, they should have lived happily ever after, but unfortunately, one thing about Heng O made this impossible. She was intelligent and beautiful and lots of fun, but she was more curious then a million cats! That's how she had broken the vase at the Jade Emperor's palace; she was so eager to see what was inside that she knocked it over.

Hou Yi loved his wife very much, but he was sure that her curiosity would get her into trouble one day. "Oh, nonsense," Heng O sniffed. "What's wrong with being interested in things, hmm?"

The two lived happily together until one day when something very strange happened. Instead of just one sun rising in the morning, TEN suns rose, each one hotter then the last! In the span of an hour, all of the crops were scorched. People were being sunburned, and it was so hot all of the rivers dried up! Hou Yi knew someone had to do something about this before the whole land became a fireball, so he took his magical arrows and carefully shot down all of the suns except one. The sky became blue again and all the people cheered with relief.

The Jade Emperor heard how Hou Yi had saved his people, and so he descended from his heavenly court to reward him. "To think, a mortal has accomplished something this extraordinary!" he said to himself.

When he got to Hou Yi's house, the first thing he saw was Heng O. He remembered her from his court, and she yelped and ran into the house. The Jade Emperor swept in after her.

"Hou Yi, I have heard about your wonderful archery skills and how you saved the land. I am forever grateful for your help."

Hou Yi was amazed that the Jade Emperor had actually descended to speak to him! He offered him all of the benefits of his household and tried to make him as comfortable as possible. "Jade Emperor, your presence is an honor! I only wish my wife, Heng O, was here to see you!" he explained.

The Jade Emperor smiled. "As a reward for your good deed, I have decided to give you the Elixir of Life!" He carefully placed a small bottle of liquid on the table. "Drink this bottle up, and you will ascend to the heavenly court, where you will live forever!"

Hou Yi gasped. He had never been granted such an honor before. Still, he might miss his home on earth.

As if reading his thoughts, the Jade Emperor said, "There are only two conditions. Do not drink the elixir until a year from today. This will give you plenty of time to learn if you are ready to say good-bye to earth and live forever in the heavens. And second, do not tell your wife about this. Her curiosity has not gone unnoticed by me!"

The Jade Emperor left Hou Yi's house and he carefully hid the bottle under a rafter in the roof. He didn't like hiding anything from Heng O, but he knew the emperor was right.

The year passed quickly and Hou Yi was still undecided about drinking the elixir. One day, he went out, and Heng O decided to clean the house from top to bottom. She began dusting under the rafters using a tall ladder, and before she got very far, she discovered the little bottle containing the elixir.

I wonder what this is, she thought, swirling the liquid in the bottle. *Who would have put this bottle in such a strange place? Hou Yi probably hid it because he wanted to keep this all to himself.* She sniffed. *Well, I'll show him. I'll drink it all up and then fill it with water so he doesn't know the difference. That'll teach that silly man.*

So, she began to drink the elixir, and as she did, she got the strangest sensation. She felt her body getting lighter, and start to float. But just as she had drunk half the elixir, Hou Yi came in and saw what she was doing.

"Heng O, don't do it!" He called up to her. He startled her so much that she dropped the bottle and it shattered, spilling half the elixir all over the floor. Heng O floated up to the ceiling and began to slide to the window.

"See what your curiosity has done!" Hou Yi shouted up to her angrily.

"Well, it would never have happened if you had told me what was in the bottle," she called, just as she floated outside.

Heng O drifted up and up, but because she had only drunk half the elixir, she only reached the moon instead of the heavenly court. There she built a house and stays to this day.

Hou Yi was angry with his wife, but he began to miss her very much. The Jade Emperor realized how unhappy he was and decided to build him a house in the sun so he could be close to Heng O. Now he lives in the sun and Heng O lives in the moon. Once a year during autumn, when Heng O's full-moon house is the brightest, Hou Yi visits his wife. This is when the Chinese people celebrate the Moon Festival and families reunite, just like the separated couple in the heavens.

My Bed is a Boat

My bed is like a little boat;
Nurse helps me in when I embark;
She girds me in my sailor's coat
And starts me in the dark.

At night, I go on board and say
Good night to all my friends on shore;
I shut my eyes and sail away
And see and hear no more.

And sometimes things to bed I take,
As prudent sailors have to do;
Perhaps a slice of wedding cake,
Perhaps a toy or two.

All night across the dark we steer;
But when the day returns at last,
Safe in my room, beside the pier,
I find my vessel fast.

—Robert Louis Stevenson

The Cricket in

"Harry, suppose we take Chester up and show him Times Square. Would you like that, Chester?"

"I guess so," said Chester, although he was really a little leery of venturing out into New York City.

The three of them jumped down to the floor. The crack in the side of the newsstand was just wide enough for Harry to get through. As they crossed the station floor, Tucker pointed out the local sights of interest, such as the Nedick's lunch counter—Tucker spent a lot of time around there—and the Loft's candy store. Then they came to the drain pipe. Chester had to make short little hops to keep from hitting his head as they went up. There seemed to be hundreds of twistings and turnings, and many other pipes that opened off the main route, but Tucker Mouse knew his way perfectly—even in the dark. At last Chester saw light above them. One more hop brought him out onto the sidewalk. And there he gasped, holding his breath and crouching against the cement.

They were standing at one corner of the Times building, which is at the south end of Times Square. Above the cricket, towers that seemed like mountains of light rose up into the night sky. Even this late the neon signs were still blazing. Reds, blues, greens and yellows flashed down on him. And the air was full of the roar of traffic and the hum of human beings. It was as if Times Square were a kind of shell, with colors and noises breaking in great waves inside it. Chester's heart hurt him and he closed his eyes. The sight was too terrible and beautiful for a cricket who up to now had measured high things by

Times Square

George Selden

the height of his willow tree and sounds by the burble of a running brook.

"How do you like it?" asked Tucker Mouse.

"Well—it's—it's quite something," Chester stuttered.

"You should see it New Year's Eve," said Harry Cat.

Gradually, Chester's eyes got used to the lights. He looked up. And way far above them, above New York, and above the whole world, he made out a star that he knew was a star he used to look at back in Connecticut. When they had gone down to the station and Chester was in the matchbox again, he though about that star. It made him feel better to think that there was one familiar thing, twinkling above him, amidst so much that was new and strange. ☾

BRIGHT

There's no need to be afraid of the dark when you brighten up your night with these illuminating crafts. You'll be amazed at how easy it is to turn a plain old lamp into something extraordinary. Make a glow-in-the-dark lamp shade, and then switch off the light for a hidden surprise! Or make a pretty, bright stained-glass lantern.

Glow-In-the-Dark Lamp Shade

Smooth white lamp shade (from a home supply store; look for one that doesn't have a finish), narrow paintbrush, wide paintbrush, light-colored fabric paint (for base color), fabric paint in assorted colors, paper plate, sponges cut into small shapes (stars, moons, etc.), glow-in-the-dark clear paint or glaze

1. Using the wide paintbrush, paint the whole lamp shade with the light-colored fabric paint. This will be the background color. Wait until the lamp shade is completely dry.
2. Pour a little bit of fabric paint onto the paper plate. Press sponges into the paint. Decorate the lamp shade by pressing the sponges firmly and carefully on to the surface. You can also paint on different shapes using a paintbrush.
3. Wait until the shapes are dry, then use the narrow paintbrush to go over the shapes with glow-in-the-dark clear paint or glaze.
4. Allow the lamp shade to dry, then put it on the lamp. Admire the cool patterns and let the paint absorb the light, then flip the lights off and see what suddenly appears!

Stained-Glass Lantern

Newspaper, white glue, 2 glass pint jars, water, tissue paper in calming colors (like purple, blue, and soft yellow), scissors, paintbrush, small fat candle

1. Lay down newspaper to work on.
2. Squeeze glue into one jar until the bottom is completely covered. Slowly add water and mix until it looks milky.
3. Cut shapes of different sizes out of the colored tissue paper.
4. Brush a section of the outside of the second

jar with the glue solution.

5. Place the tissue paper shapes on the glue section. Try arranging the shapes in different ways and overlapping the pieces a little bit.

6. Repeat the process of brushing on some glue and then adding the tissue paper shapes until the outside of the jar is completely covered. Let it dry.

7. Place a small, fat candle in the bottom of the jar and have a grown-up light it. Watch the room fill with color when the flame sends shadows dancing!

NOTE: Always use the lantern with parental supervision, and always remember to blow the candle out before you go to sleep or leave the room.

Moon-catchin' Net

I've made me a moon-catchin' net,
And I'm goin' huntin' tonight,
I'll run along swingin' it over my head,
And grab for that big ball of light.

So tomorrow just look at the sky,
And if there's no moon you can bet
I've found what I sought and I finally caught
The moon in my moon-catchin' net.

But if the moon's still shinin' there,
Look close underneath and you'll get
A clear look at me in the sky swingin' free
With a star in my moon-catchin' net.

—*Shel Silverstein*

Afraid of the Dark

I'm Reginald Clark, I'm afraid of the dark
So I always insist on the light on,
And my teddy to hug,
And my blanket to rub,
And my thumby to suck or to bite on.
And three bedtime stories,
Two trips to the toilet,
Two prayers, and five hugs from my mommy,
I'm Reginald Clark, I'm afraid of the dark
So please do not close this book on me.

—*Shel Silverstein*

Angel of God, my guardian dear,
to whom God's love commits me here;
Watch over me throughout the night,
keep me safe within your sight.

—*Traditional*

May it be delightful my house;
From my head may it be delightful;
To my feet may it be delightful;
Where I lie may it be delightful;
All above me may it be delightful;
All around me may it be delightful.

—*Navajo*

Selene and Endymion

Once upon a time, there lived a goddess who guided the moon across the sky each evening. Her name was Selene, and she was the brightest goddess on Mount Olympus, the home of the gods. Every evening she would emerge from her home, then drift across the sky with the silvery orb and look down on all the sleeping people of the world. She saw families snuggled together in houses. Little animals were curled up in burrows and fields. Birds snoozed with their heads tucked under their wings. Even fish burbled sleepily in the streams and rivers. It made her happy to see so many peaceful images.

One night, she looked down and saw a small group of sheep clustered around a lone figure. She drifted a bit closer to the ground and saw that it was Endymion, the shepherd, quietly sleeping under a tree. He looked so peaceful and content that Selene stopped right in the middle of the sky to gaze at him. She wondered what kind of dreams he was having. Then she remembered where she was and floated with the moon toward the other end of the earth. But she didn't forget Endymion.

From then on, she would look for Endymion every night as she traveled through the heavens. And every night she would find him sweetly sleeping in his glade. Now, Endymion must not have been a very good shepherd, since he was too busy napping to keep an eye on his flock. Luckily, Selene asked the spirits of the trees, the dryads, to watch over him and sing lullabies to make sure his sheep didn't wander. Sometimes Selene would rise a bit early, just to spend a few minutes more looking down on Endymion. After a while, it seemed to take longer and longer for the moon to make its way across the globe and then disappear so the sun could rise.

As for Endymion, during this time he had the most wonderful dreams. He dreamed of laughing women singing to his sheep, and of roaming the countryside on the wings of the wind. But most of all, he dreamed of a very lovely woman with dark, smooth skin and silver-streaked hair. Little did he know, he was actually dreaming of Selene!

Zeus began to notice that the moon was taking longer and longer to travel across the sky each night. One evening, he transformed himself into a mighty eagle to investigate the problem. He found Selene floating stock-still, holding the silvery moon and gazing down with love   at sleeping Endymion.

"Selene, I've been hearing complaints from all over. Apollo is mad because he never knows when the sun will rise. No one is waking up on time because you keep taking too long with the moon," he scolded her.

The moon goddess sighed. "I know, but I can't help it. I see Endymion sleeping, and I can't tear myself away." She gave another heavy sigh, "He is so young and beautiful, and yet I'm sad because one day he will be old and not able to come to the grove of trees with his sheep anymore." A small tear trickled from her eye. "I wish he could stay this young forever. Is it possible for one of the humans to become immortal, like us gods?"

Zeus glided around her in eagle form. "It's possible, but unfortunately, Endymion would fall into the everlasting sleep. He would never grow old or sick, but he would also never wake up."

Selene thought about this as she gazed at the solitary shepherd. She couldn't bear to think of him leaving the grove, but at the same time, she knew that she would never be able to talk or laugh with him as he dozed forever. Finally, she nodded her head.

"I would rather Endymion sleep forever than lose him one day," she decided.

Zeus swooped down to the earth and quickly gathered some magical herbs and objects: nightshade, stardust, an owl's feather, and a drop of water from Styx, the river that ran through the Underworld. He mixed them together to make a potion and sprinkled it lightly on Endymion's face. Endymion sighed in his sleep and then rolled over, caught forever in eternal slumber.

"Oh, thank you!" said Selene, swooping down and placing a kiss on Endymion's soft cheek. Then she returned to complete her trip across the night sky.

And to this day, Endymion sleeps in the green glade, eternally watched over with adoring eyes by Selene, the moon goddess. Sometimes she will send moonbeams down like kisses to fall on his sleeping face. He has the most fantastic dreams as the moon travels through the sky, but his favorite is the one in which he happily walks with Selene, the beautiful silver maiden, forever and ever.

Night

The sun descending in the west,
The evening star does shine;
The birds are silent in their nest,
And I must seek for mine.

The moon like a flower
In heaven's high bower,
With silent delight,
Sits and smiles on the night.

—William Blake

Twelve Dancing Princesses

Once upon a time there was a king who had twelve beautiful daughters. The princesses slept side by side in twelve beds. Each night when they went to bed, the king shut and locked their door. But each morning he opened the door to find that their shoes had been danced to pieces, and nobody could explain how it happened.

So the king announced that anyone who discovered where the princesses secretly danced in the night could choose one of them to be his wife and would inherit the kingdom. But whoever tried and failed to make the discovery after three days and nights would be put to death.

A prince soon appeared and offered to take the risk. At night, he was taken to the chamber next to the one where the princesses slept in their twelve beds. The doors of both chambers were left open so that the princesses could not leave without being seen. But the prince's eyes grew heavy, and he fell asleep on his watch. When he woke in the morning, all the princesses had been dancing. The soles of their shoes were full of holes. The second and third evenings passed with the same result, and the prince lost his head. Many others came after him and offered to take the chance, but they all lost their lives.

One day, an old soldier passed through the kingdom. On his travels he met an old woman who asked him where he was going. "I hardly know myself," said the soldier, and added jokingly, "I'd like to discover where the twelve princesses dance, and become king."

"Well, that's not very hard to do," said the old woman. "Don't drink any of the wine the princesses serve in the evening. Then, as soon as they leave you, pretend to be fast asleep."

The old woman gave him a cloak and said, "When you wear this, you will be invisible. Follow the princesses wherever they go." Once the soldier heard all this good advice, he was determined to try his luck.

He was welcomed into the castle, and when the evening came he was led to the outer chamber. Just as he was going to lie down, the eldest of the princesses brought him a cup of wine. The soldier had tied a sponge beneath his chin, and he let the wine run into it. He didn't drink a drop. Then he lay down on his bed, and in a little while began to snore very loudly. When the twelve princesses heard this they laughed, and the eldest said, "This fellow, too, might have done better things with his life!" They groomed themselves in front of their mirrors, and skipped about, eager to begin dancing.

Sure that they were quite safe, the eldest went up to her own bed and clapped her hands, and the bed sunk into the floor. The soldier saw them going down through the opening one after another, the eldest leading the way. With no time to lose, he jumped up, put on the invisible cloak, and followed them. But in the middle of the stairs he stepped on the corner of the youngest princess's dress, causing her to cry out to her sisters, "Someone grabbed at my dress."

"You silly creature!" said the eldest. "You caught it on a nail." Then down they all went, and at the bottom they found themselves in a most delightful orchard. The leaves on the trees were silver, and glittered and sparkled. The soldier wished to take away some token of the place; so he broke off a little branch. Snap!

"Did you hear that noise?" asked the youngest sister. "Something is terribly wrong."

"It is only our princes, who are shouting for joy at our approach," said the eldest.

Then they came to another orchard, where all the leaves on the trees were gold; and afterward to a third, where the leaves were all glittering diamonds. The soldier broke a branch from each; and every time there was a loud noise, which made the youngest sister tremble with fear. Snap! Crack! But the eldest still said it was only the princes, who were crying for joy. So they went on until they came to a great lake; and at the side of the lake were twelve little boats with twelve handsome princes in them.

The princesses got into their boats, and the soldier stepped into the same boat with the youngest. As they were rowing over the lake, her prince said, "I don't understand it, but the boat seems much heavier today."

"It is only the heavy heat," said the princess.

On the other side of the lake stood a beautiful, brightly lit palace. When the boats landed, everyone rushed up the palace steps. Each prince danced with his princess, and the invisible soldier danced among them; and when any of the princesses had a cup of wine set by her, he drank it all up, so that when she put the cup to her mouth it was empty. At this, too, the youngest sister was horribly frightened, but the eldest always silenced her. They danced until three o'clock in the morning, and then all their shoes were worn out. So, the princes rowed them back over the lake; but this time the soldier placed himself in the boat with the eldest princess. On the opposite shore, the princesses said good-bye to their princes.

As they approached the staircase, the soldier quickly ran ahead to his room and lay down. The sisters heard the soldier snoring in his bed. They said, "We are safe." In the morning, the soldier said nothing about what had happened. He wanted to see more of this strange adventure, and went again the second and third nights. Everything happened just as before; however, on the third night, the soldier carried away one of the golden cups as a token of where he had been.

Finally, the soldier was taken before the king to tell what he knew. He brought the three branches and the golden cup. The king asked him where his twelve daughters danced at night. The soldier told the king all that had happened and showed him the three branches and the golden cup. The king called for the princesses, and asked them if what the soldier said was true. They confessed, and the king asked the soldier which daughter he would choose for his wife.

He answered, "I am not very young, so I will have the eldest."

They were married that very day, and the soldier was chosen to be the king's successor.

The Phantom

The sun was dropping slowly from sight, and stripes of purple and orange and crimson and gold piled themselves on top of the distant hills. The last shafts of light waited patiently for a flight of wrens to find their way home, and a group of anxious stars had already taken their places.

"Here we are!" cried Alec, and, with a sweep of his arm, he pointed toward an enormous symphony orchestra. "Isn't it a grand sight?"

There were at least a thousand musicians ranged in a great arc before them. To the left and right were the violins and cellos, whose bows moved in great waves, and behind them in numberless profusion the piccolos, flutes, clarinets, oboes, bassoons, horns, trumpets, trombones, and tubas were all playing at once. At the very rear, so far away that they could hardly be seen, were the percussion instruments, and lastly, in a long line up one side of a steep slope, were the solemn bass fiddles.

On a high podium in front stood the conductor, a tall, gaunt man with dark deep-set eyes and a thin mouth placed carelessly between his long pointed nose and his long

Tollbooth

Norton Juster

pointed chin. He used no baton, but conducted with large, sweeping movements which seemed to start at his toes and work slowly up through his body and along his slender arms and end finally at the tips of his graceful fingers.

"I don't hear any music," said Milo.

"That's right," said Alec; "you don't listen to this concert—you watch it. Now, pay attention."

As the conductor waved his arms, he molded the air like handfuls of soft clay, and his musicians carefully followed his every direction.

"What are they playing?" asked Tock, looking up inquisitively at Alec.

"The sunset, of course. They play it every evening, about this time."

"They do?" said Milo quizzically.

"Naturally," answered Alec; "and they also play morning, noon, and night, when, of course, it's morning, noon, or night. Why, there wouldn't be any color in the world unless they played it. Each instrument plays a different one," he explained, "and depending, of course, on what season it is and how the weather's to be, the conductor chooses his score and directs the day. But watch: the sun has almost set, and in a moment you can ask Chroma himself."

The last colors slowly faded from the western sky, and, as they did, one by one the instruments stopped, until only the bass fiddles, in their somber slow movement, were left to play the night and a single set of silver bells brightened the constellations. The conductor let his arms fall limply at his sides and stood quite still as darkness claimed the forest.

"That was a very beautiful sunset," said Milo, walking to the podium.

"It should be," was the reply; "we've been practicing since the world began." And, reaching down, the speaker picked Milo off the ground and set him on the music stand. "I am Chroma the Great," he continued, gesturing broadly with his hands, "conductor of color, maestro of pigment, and director of the entire spectrum."

"Do you play all day long?" asked Milo when he had introduced himself.

"Ah yes, all day, every day," he sang out, then pirouetted gracefully around the platform. "I rest only at night, and even then *they* play on."

"What would happen if you stopped?" asked Milo, who didn't quite believe that color happened that way.

"See for yourself!" roared Chroma, and he raised both hands high over his head. Immediately the instruments that were playing stopped, and at once all color vanished.

The world looked like an enormous coloring book that had never been used. Everything appeared in simple black outlines, and it looked as if someone with a set of paints the size of a house and a brush as wide could stay happily occupied for years. Then Chroma lowered his arms. The instruments began again and the color returned.

"You see what a dull place the world would be without color?" he said, bowing until his chin almost touched the ground. "But what pleasure to lead my violins in a serenade of spring green or hear my trumpets blare out the blue sea and then watch the oboes tint it all in warm yellow sunshine. And rainbows are best of all—and blazing neon signs, and taxicabs with stripes, and the soft, muted tones of a foggy day. We play them all."

As Chroma spoke, Milo sat with his eyes open wide, and Alec, Tock, and the Humbug looked on in wonder.

"Now I really must get some sleep." Chroma yawned. "We've had lighting, fireworks, and parades for the last few nights, and I've had to be up to conduct them. But tonight is sure to be quiet." Then, putting his large hand on Milo's shoulder, he said, "Be a good fellow and watch my orchestra till morning, will you? And be sure to wake me at 5:23 for the sunrise. Good night, good night, good night."

With that he leaped lightly from the podium and, in three long steps, vanished into the forest.

"That's a good idea," said Tock, making himself comfortable in the grass as the bug grumbled himself quickly to sleep and Alec stretched out in mid-air.

And Milo, full of thoughts and questions, curled up on the pages of tomorrow's music and eagerly awaited the dawn. ☾

GALACTIC

Our solar system is made up of the sun and the nine planets, as well as many moons, asteroids, stars, and comets. Using household items, glue, paint, and a little imagination you can create your own mini-galaxy to enjoy as you drift off to sleep. Decorate your room with this out-of-this-world mobile and learn facts about each planet's appearance.

Markers, cardboard, scissors, aluminum foil, hole punch, string, glue, glitter, yellow plastic container lid, four yellow or orange pipe cleaners, Styrofoam balls, paint, paintbrush, toothpicks, plastic lid, large needle, thread, two sticks about a foot long

Moon
1. Draw a crescent or full moon on cardboard. Cut out and wrap with aluminum foil.
2. Punch a hole near the top. Thread string through and attach to the mobile base.

Stars
1. Draw different-sized stars on cardboard. Make some with longer and shorter points.
2. Spread a thin layer of glue on top and sprinkle each with a different color glitter. Let dry. Repeat on other side.
3. Punch a hole near the end of a point. Thread string through and tie to mobile base.

Sun
1. Cut eight small equally spaced slits along the rim of the yellow plastic lid.

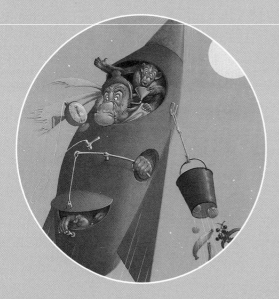

MOBILE

2. Bend each pipe cleaner into a V-shape, and slip the two ends into a slit. You should have the bent part sticking out to form triangular sunbeams all around the lid edge.

3. Thread a piece of string through one of the top triangles and attach to mobile base.

Planets

1. Create the nine planets using different-sized Styrofoam balls and paint. Design each of the planets with a different characteristic:

Mercury is half the size of Earth, making it the second smallest planet in the solar system. It has a gray surface.

★ Venus is about the size of Earth and has a thick cloud cover that reflects sunlight and makes it appear white.

★ Earth is medium-sized, with water and clouds on the planet's surface, making it appear blue with white swirls.

★ Mars is smaller than Earth and has a fiery red color.

★ Jupiter is the largest planet and has swirls of brown, white, gray, and blue.

★ Saturn is encircled by thin, prominent rings. Create the rings by inserting two toothpicks opposite from each other on each side of a ball. Cut out the center of a plastic lid, leaving enough room for the planet, and then slip on top of the toothpicks to create the ring.

★ Uranus is a large planet. Methane gases in the atmosphere cause it to appear blue-green.

★ Neptune contains a layer of cold water around its core that moves to the surface and becomes a gas, giving the large planet a bluish color.

★ Pluto is the smallest planet in the solar system. It appears gray.

2. To hang, have a grown-up thread a large needle with thread and knot it. Push the needle through the bottom of the planet so it comes out the top. The knot should catch on the bottom. Tie to the mobile.

Mobile Base

1. Use string to bind the two sticks together in the middle so they make an X-shape.

2. Attach a string from the center of the X so you can hang the mobile.

3. Tie on moon, sun, stars, and planets!

I believe in the sun
even when it is not shining.
I believe in love
even when feeling it not.
I believe in God
even when He is silent.

—*Jewish*

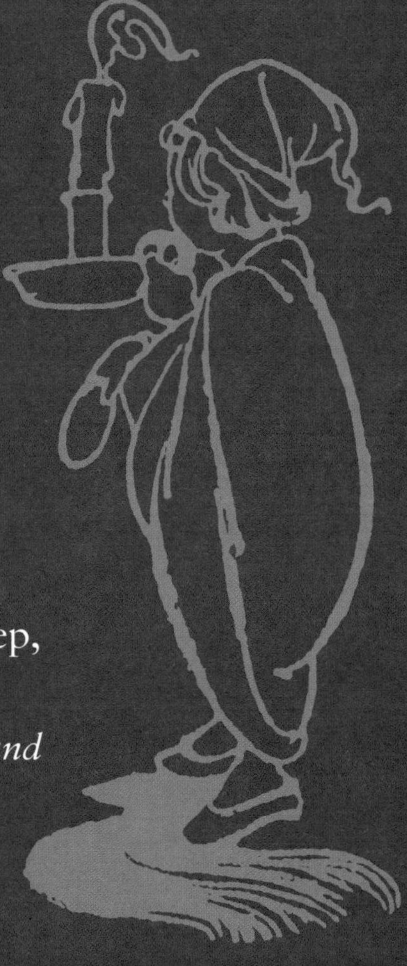

*L*ord, keep us safe this night,
Secure from all our fears;
May angels guard us while we sleep,
Till morning light appears.

—*John Leland*

URSA MAJOR
BIG DIPPER

Regulus

LEO LION

the SUMMER SKY *looking north*

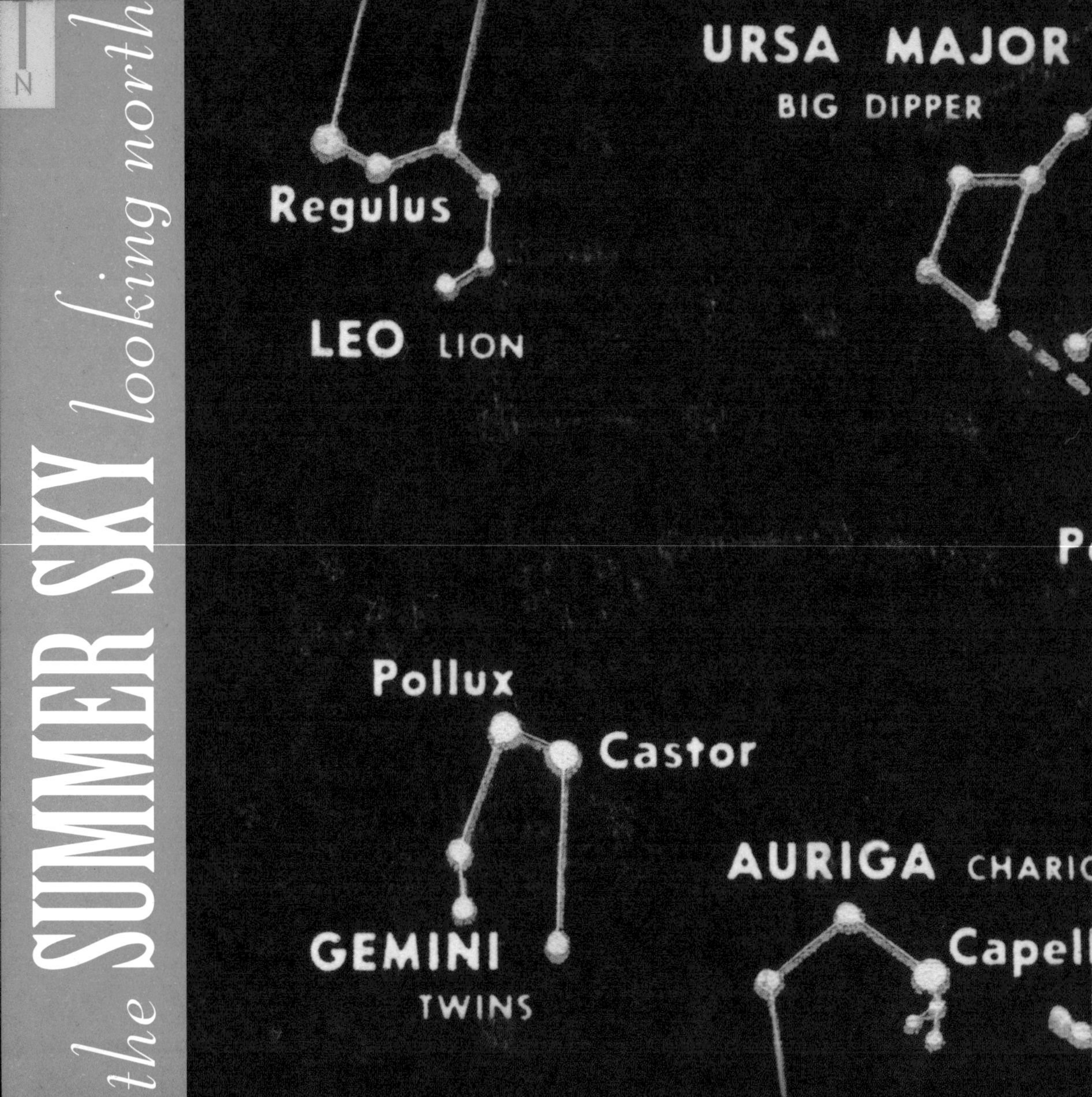

Pollux

Castor

GEMINI
TWINS

AURIGA CHARIO

Capell

Mizar

DRACO DRAGON

LYRA

Vega

CYGNUS

SWAN

MINOR

LITTLE DIPPER

Deneb

laris

Pole Star

CEPHEUS

CASSIOPEIA

EER

PERSEUS

S

the **SUMMER SKY** *looking south*

Vega

LYRA
LYRE

HERCULE

CO
NORTH

Altair

AQUILA
EAGLE

OPHIUCHUS
SERPENT

SAGITTARIUS
ARCHER

Antares

BOÖTES

COMA BERENICES
BERENICE'S HAIR

ONA
N CROWN   Arcturus

LEO LION

Regulus

EARER

VIRGO

VIRGIN

LIBRA
SCALES

Spica

CORVUS
CROW

CORPIO

SCORPION

CENTAURUS

the **WINTER SKY** *looking north*

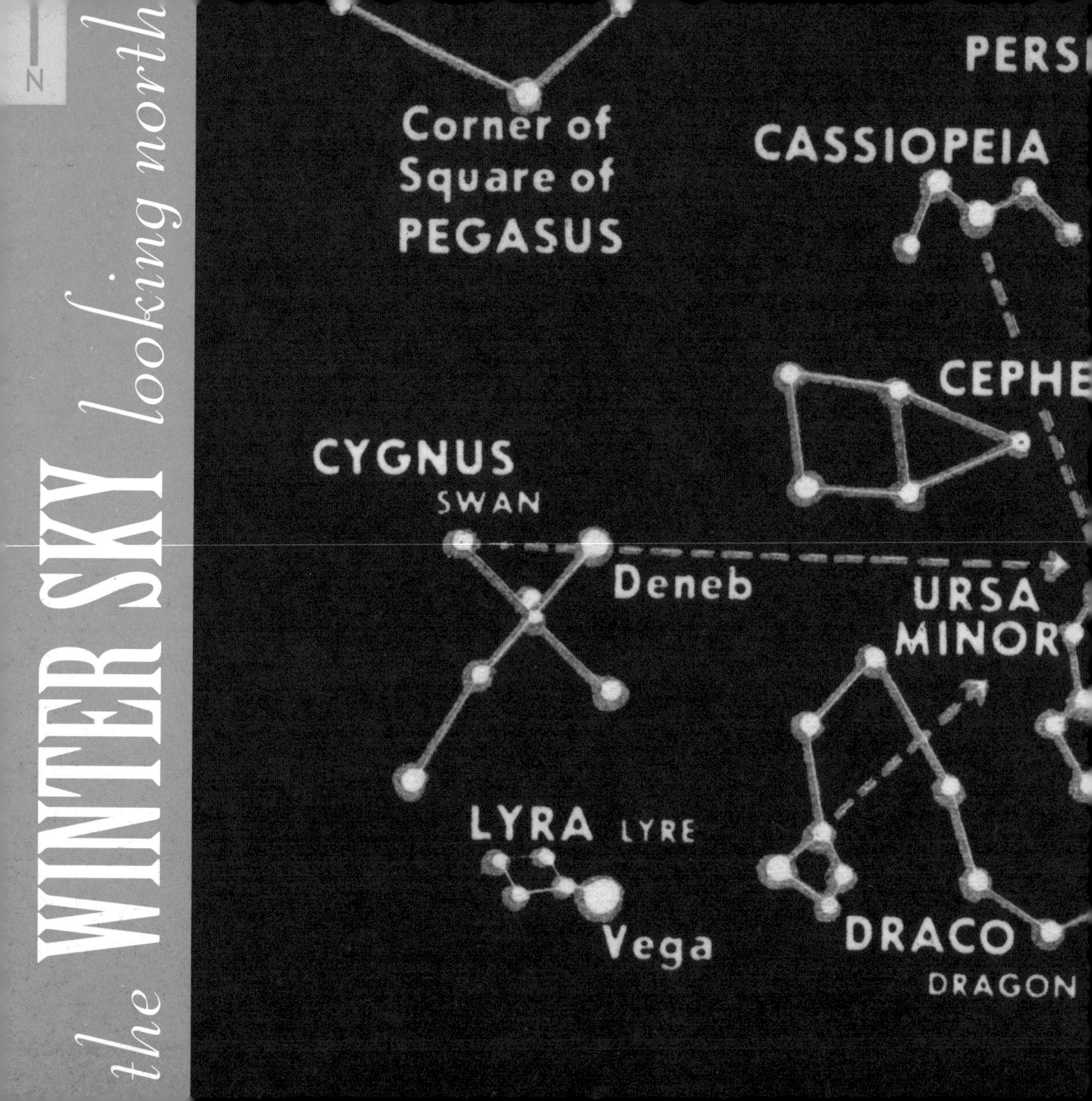

Corner of
Square of
PEGASUS

CASSIOPEIA

PERSE

CEPHE

CYGNUS
SWAN

Deneb

**URSA
MINOR**

LYRA LYRE

Vega

DRACO
DRAGON

S

The
Kids AURIGA

Capella

GEMINI
TWINS

Castor
Pollux

S

Polaris Pole Star

TTLE
DIPPER

URSA MAJOR
BIG DIPPER

LEO
LION

Mizar

↓
S

the WINTER SKY *looking south*

Capella · The Kids

AURIGA
CHARIOTEER

Castor
Pollux
GEMINI
TWINS

Plei...
Sever...

Aldebaran

TAURU...
BULL

Betelgeuze

Procyon
CANIS MINOR
LITTLE DOG

ORION

Rigel

Sirius
BIG DOG

CANIS
MAJOR

LEPUS HARE

COLUMBA DOVE

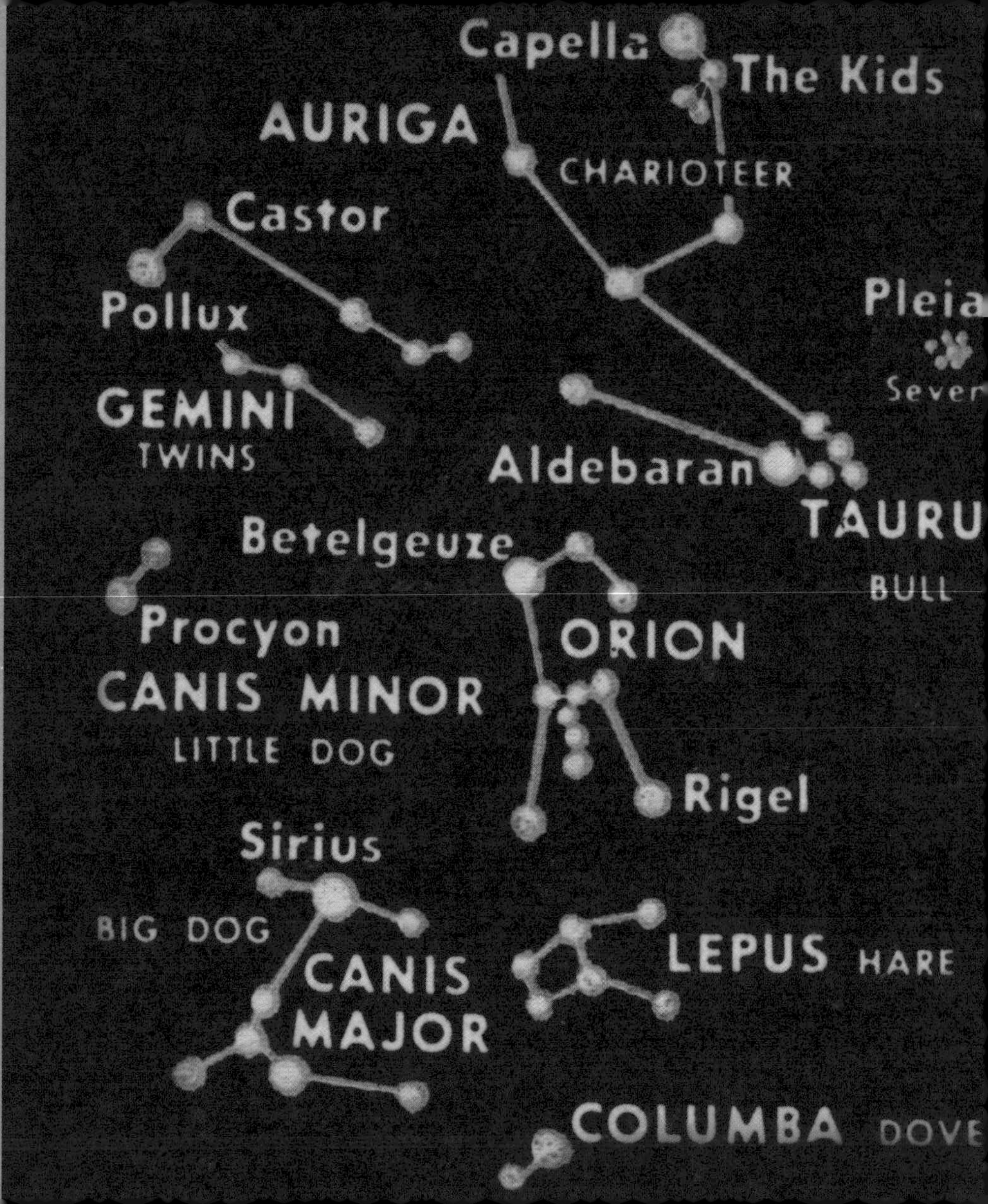

ANDROMEDA

Algol

PEGASUS

ARIES
RAM

Great
Square

PISCES FISHES

CETUS
WHALE

AQUARIUM
WATER BEARER

Fomalhaut

Published in 2005 by Welcome Books®
An imprint of Welcome Enterprises, Inc.
6 West 18th Street, New York, NY 10011
(212) 989-3200, Fax (212) 989-3205
www.welcomebooks.com

Publisher: Lena Tabori
Project Director: Alice Wong
Designer: Naomi Irie
Tales and Legends retold by Deidra Garcia and Alice Wong
Recipes and Activities text by Deidra Garcia and Alice Wong
Line illustrations for Activities by Kathryn Shaw

Front jacket illustration by Victor C. Anderson

Distributed to the trade in the U.S. and Canada by
Andrews McMeel Distribution Services
U.S. Order Department and Customer Service Toll-free: (800) 943-9839
U.S. Orders-only Fax: (800) 943-9831
PUBNET S&S San Number: 200-2442
Canada Orders Toll-free: (800) 268-3216
Canada Order-only Fax: (888) 849-8151

Library of Congress Cataloging-in-Publication Data on file.

ISBN 1-932183-72-8

Printed in China

FIRST EDITION
10 9 8 7 6 5 4 3 2 1

ACKNOWLEDGMENTS

★"who knows if the moon's" Copyright 1923, 1925, 1951, 1953, © 1991 by the Trustees for the E. E. Cummings Trust. Copyright © 1976 by George James Firmage, from COMPLETE POEMS: 1904-1962 by E. E. Cummings, edited by George J. Firmage. Used by permission of Liveright Publishing Corporation.

★From JAMES AND THE GIANT PEACH by Roald Dahl, copyright © 1961, renewed 1989 by Roald Dahl Nominee Limited. Used by permission of Alfred A. Knopf, an imprint of Random House Children's Books, a division of Random House, Inc.

★From THE PHANTOM TOLLBOOTH by Norton Juster, copyright © 1961, and renewed 1989 by Norton Juster. Used by permission of Random House Children's Books, a division of Random House, Inc.

★"Dream a Little Dream of Me" Lyrics by Gus Kahn, Music by Wilbur Schwandt and Fabrian Andree. © Copyright 1930 (Renewed),1931 (Renewed), Essex Music Inc., Words and Music, Inc. New York, Don Swan Publications, Miami, Florida and Gilbert Keyes Music, Hollywood, California.

★"Good Night" by John Lennon and Paul McCartney. © 1968 Sony/ATV Tunes LLC. All rights administered by Sony/ATV Music Publishing, 8 Music Square West, Nashville, TN 37203. All rights reserved. International Copyright Secured. Used by permission.

★"I'm Only Sleeping" by John Lennon and Paul McCartney. © 1966 Sony/ATV Tunes LLC. All rights administered by Sony/ATV Music Publishing, 8 Music Square West, Nashville, TN 37203. All rights reserved. International Copyright Secured. Used by permission.

★"Moon River" from the Paramount Picture BREAKFAST AT TIFFANY'S. Words by Johnny Mercer, Music by Henry Mancini. Copyright © 1961 (Renewed 1989) by Famous Music Corporation. International Copyright Secured. All Rights Reserved.

★"Night Creature" from LITTLE RACOON AND POEMS FROM THE WOODS by Lilian Moore. Copyright © 1975 by Lilian Moore. Used by permission of Marian Reiner for the author.

★"Most Beds are Beds" from THE BED BOOK by Sylvia Plath. Text copyright © 1976 by Ted Hughes. Used by permission of HarperCollins Publishers.

★Excerpt from THE LITTLE PRINCE by Antoine de Saint-Exupéry, English translation copyright © 1943 by Harcourt, Inc. and renewed 1971 by Consuelo de Saint-Exupéry, English translation copyright © 2000 by Richard Howard, reprinted by permission of Harcourt, Inc.

★From THE CRICKET IN TIMES SQUARE by George Selden, copyright © 1960. Reprinted by permission of Farrar, Straus and Giroux, LLC.

★"Afraid of the Dark" by Shel Silverstein. Copyright © 1974 by Evil Eye Music, Inc. Used by permission of HarperCollins Publishers.

★"Moon-catchin' Net" by Shel Silverstein. Copyright © 1981 by Evil Eye Music, Inc. Used by permission of HarperCollins Publishers.

★"St. Judy's Comet" Copyright © 1973 Paul Simon. Used by permission of Paul Simon Music.

★Excerpt from MARY POPPINS copyright © 1934 and renewed 1962 by P. L. Travers, reprinted by permission of Harcourt, Inc.

★"When You Wish Upon a Star" Words by Ned Washington, Music by Leigh Harline. © Copyright 1940 by Bourne Co. Copyright Renewed. All Rights Reserved. International Copyright Secured.

★"Flying" by J.M. Westrup from A BOOK OF A THOUSAND POEMS, Evans Brothers Publishers.

★From CHARLOTTE'S WEB by E.B. White. Copyright © 1952 by E. B. White. Text copyright © renewed 1980 by E.B. White. Reprinted by permission of HarperCollins Publishers.

ILLUSTRATIONS

Pg. 10, 22: Margaret Evans Price; pg. 14-15 Henriette Willebeek Le Mair; pg. 35, 61: Vernon Thomas; pg. 41, 135, 153, 166-167: Anne Anderson; pg. 50, 150-151, 187: Jessie Willcox Smith; pg. 53: Adina Sand; pg. 54: Frederick Richardson; pg. 68: N. Dowdall; pg. 78: Raphael Kirchner; pg. 86-87: Paul Bransom; pg. 96: Maxfield Parrish; pg. 98: George Senseney; pg. 100-101, 174: Blanche Fisher Wright; pg. 106: Barham; pg. 109: Torrey; pg. 122: Emily Gertrude Thomson; pg. 131: E. Nash; pg. 139: Charlotte Becker; pg. 140-141: S. Beatrice Pearse; pg. 145: W. W. Denslow; pg. 149: Maud Humphrey; pg. 163, 183: F. Bisel Peat; pg. 181: Gustav Michelson; pg. 192: Coby; pg. 197: Stephen W. Meader; pg. 204-205: Willie Pogany; pg. 210: Lawson Wood; pg. 212: Katherine Gassaway

"Thank the lord you are well!
And now go to sleep!"
said Miss Clavel.
and she turned out the light—
And closed the door—
and that's all there is—
there isn't anymore.

—*Madeline*, Ludwig Bemelmans